# The Music of Humanity

## Shawn Merritt

# The Music of Humanity

Shawn Merritt

RIVER BIRCH PRESS

Daphne, Alabama

ISBN 978-1-956365-23-8  (print)
ISBN 978-1-956365-24-5  (e-book)

For Worldwide Distribution
Printed in the U.S.A.

River Birch Press
P.O. Box 868, Daphne, AL 36526

# Introduction

I began writing this book about fifteen years ago when I was struggling with depression, anxiety, an addiction to drugs, and alcoholism. I wasted my days getting high to escape the pain and wrote at night when I came home from partying. The first fourteen chapters, roughly seventy-five percent of the book, reflect this lifestyle. I think you will find it to be a very poetic, yet painful reflection of my life at the time. You will see firsthand what it is like to struggle in such a devastating and profound way.

So, thinking I had told a full story of my pain at the time, I self-published the book under the title *The Still Sad Music*, but little did I know it was quite incomplete. It sold very few copies because it was merely a tale of depression and disillusionment. There was no redemption for my main character, Jeffrey Killingsworth, and there was no redemption for myself at the time, either.

I got saved roughly five years ago and began to explore writing the book again a few years later. I felt there was something more to add. My salvation caused me to look at the world in a very different light. Consequently, I wanted to add a story of redemption at the end of the book. And I wanted my readers to feel redeemed themselves as they partook in the life of my main character.

It took me nearly two years to add an additional three chapters. I wanted it to be perfect, so I worked slowly and tried to put down onto paper the changes that had occurred in my own life. As you read the first two of these three chapters, I think that you will find them as life-changing as they are for me. Perhaps you will even be saved, provided you are not already.

I think you will find the last chapter to be a metaphorical walk beside the still waters. As Jeffrey Killingsworth proceeds in his walk of faith, he studies what God has said about the peace that is found in Jesus Christ our Lord. His journey from drugs to salvation culminates perfectly in this chapter. I think that as you read it, you will also find the peace of God that passes all understanding and fills us with a purpose in life.

This is now a story of redemption that can only occur through salvation. It isn't merely a story of correcting one's life or getting clean. It is a story about a drastic and magnificent change in meaning and purpose for the life of my main character—and myself.

# 1

"I think I may be losing it," mumbled the teary-eyed boy sitting lazily by the window in his otherwise unoccupied room. Like a premature hand-me-down, his raggedy Legends of the NFL pajamas hung loosely about his scrawny frame, extending well past his feet and onto the floor, where they collected dirt and dust with amazing proficiency. On his pajama collar, *Property of Jeffrey Killingsworth* was written in red fluorescent ink.

It had lately become a habit of his mother to place labels like this on every article of clothing he owned, from T-shirts and sweatpants down to the bare essentials. Jeffrey was bothered, not so much by the humiliation this habit brought on, but more so by the lunacy it revealed. After all, boys at his age were usually pretty adept at holding on to their underwear and such. Nevertheless, Jeffrey wore his property with pride just in case somewhere down the line he found himself lost and unconscious with no library or bus card to show his identity.

Of all his marked property, Jeffrey's favorite was the pair of pajamas that sported the greatest athletes ever to step foot upon the gridiron. From ankles to elbows, legends such as Jerry Rice, Jim Brown, and Lawrence Taylor were locked in frames of glorious motion, like cheetahs racing down hopeless prey. On the left sleeve, where Jeffrey was drying his tears, the greatest of all time, soul and skill, Walter Payton, was poised with knees high and shoulders low.

Jeffrey looked down at the majestic Chicago Bears' running

back and was immediately ashamed of the mucus and tears he had spread over the figure. *If only I could be tough and powerful like him*, Jeffrey thought as the watery snot slithered onto his top lip. *Maybe I wouldn't be so sad all the time.* He closed his eyes for a moment as if concentrating on some foreign power that granted children's wishes and then looked out the window at the sun, which was just peeking over the horizon.

On the table near Jeffrey's bed, a tired, old radio was mustering its strength for one more round. It crackled and then wheezed before Louis Armstrong could be heard scratching and scraping out the words to "What a Wonderful World."

Earlier, the hum from the radio had been nothing more than background noise, but now it was the only sound in the room as Jeffrey listened intently for his favorite part to arrive. Once Armstrong's voice reached that forbidden, orgasmic level, the clouds enrobing the rising sun suddenly wisped outward like slowly receding waters and refracted a paradisiacal orange and purple across the velvety sky.

Then, Armstrong eased into the chorus, singing, "And I think to myself...what a wonderful world." Jeffrey began to whimper lightly, and the warm, salty tears once again trickled down his soft, boyish cheeks. He was stunned by the realization that yes, it was a wonderful world, but one that excluded the strange and the troubled. He knew the flowers would never bloom for him and the colors of the rainbow would fade with every passing day.

*Maybe this is just something temporary*, Jeffrey pondered, *like a clock that falls out of sync or a ballplayer who loses his rhythm.* He began to gnaw on his fingernails, moving nervously from one to the next. *Yeah, that has to be it. Since there's nowhere to go but up, things will only get better in time.*

His reasoning was clear. He was sure of that, and as the comforting rationalizations settled in like a powerful sedative, Jeffrey felt at ease once again. He wiped the tears from his eyes and looked outside to see his father treading across the snow-covered lawn with a suitcase in each hand. It brought back memories of the way he and his dad used to throw the pigskin around during those freezing winter months.

Before Jeffrey knew it, a joyful smile was radiating from his salty lips, and he found himself actually looking forward to the day he had previously dreaded. With renewed spirits, he walked over to the pile of clothes on the floor and began rummaging for something to wear, something that would signify his newfound hope. *Maybe yellow or blue*, he pondered.

---

As the cold morning air sliced through Mr. Killingsworth's coat, an uneasy feeling swept over him. He paused for a moment to contemplate the strange sensation but then shrugged it off. *Probably just a spine chill*, he thought. It was too cold to entertain superstitious fancies anyhow, he chided himself as he quickly threw two bags into the trunk of the car, slammed it shut, and nearly sprinted toward the house.

"Dang, it just keeps getting colder every day," he mumbled to himself while shivering his way through the front door. He quickly rubbed his hands together to create a little extra warmth and then checked his watch. He and his family still had a good twenty minutes to get ready, so he relaxed a little and directed his steps toward the kitchen, where the coffee was brewing.

The antique grandfather clock at the end of the hallway gave its final resounding gong as Jeffrey came flying down the stairs in a plastic toy canoe. The small boat crashed into the wall with a tremendous force, but not before Jeffrey had the chance to bail out and release a few short bursts of laughter as his body rolled to a stop on the newly installed soft carpet. His mother, who had just entered the hallway and stopped to adjust a picture on the wall, gave a quick, angry glance at him before screaming, "Jeffrey, what on earth are you doing? You nearly went through the wall!"

"Sorry, Mom. I thought I'd be able to do a special kung fu kayak turn before I hit the wall," he mumbled while quickly wiping the grin off his face. "I'm honing my boating skills in case we decide to take a ride down the creek."

Seeing that his mother's anger had diminished to a safe level, Jeffrey stood and grabbed the canoe while briefly examining the damage he had inflicted upon the wall. "Never mind that for now," Mrs. Killingsworth said as she tried to recall her previous course of action. "We'll deal with this tonight when you get home. Now, put that canoe up and get your bag from upstairs. You did pack your bag already, didn't you?"

"Yes, ma'am," Jeffrey muttered while lowering his head in submission. Then he rested the boat on his left shoulder and hopped up the stairs like an excited young child. After fifteen long minutes had passed, he returned with a small book bag. He was layered from head to toe in what appeared to be every article of clothing he owned.

He had on so many pairs of jogging pants and sweaters that he had to walk with his arms straight out, and his legs spread wide like a mummy in a low-budget horror movie. His mother would have been frustrated with him for wasting time, but she could only laugh as she hugged him and exclaimed, "Ah! My little sumo wrestler has finally gotten chubby enough to fill out his clothes."

Mrs. Killingsworth had always been able to look upon Jeffrey's silly practical jokes in a positive manner, while most of the others were quick to spit out the word "immature." Perhaps the age of fourteen was the right time to start gaining a relatively serious outlook on life, but she had a sense that things were a little different for Jeffrey. "He's maturing a little slower than the others. No big deal," she would always tell herself. His physical appearance was certainly in support of this assumption. The growth spurt that all his peers were experiencing was nonexistent in Jeffrey.

Consequently, his clear, soft skin and innocent smile still clung to the boyish quality they had always known. Mrs. Killingsworth might have wished for Jeffrey to be more like the other kids on occasion, but she never got too worked up about it. His physical immaturity, constant daydreaming, and tendency to goof off all fell into the category she labeled as "things that would pass in time."

"Oh, that reminds me!" Mrs. Killingsworth exclaimed. "Take off some of those sweaters. I've got a surprise for you!"

She quickly turned toward the hallway and disappeared into the living room, returning in a moment with an expensive-looking black and gray coat. "The salesman said this was one of the best they had, so you're sure to keep warm."

"Thanks, Mom," Jeffrey murmured as he held the new coat before him.

For the past few months, large acts of attention toward him, such as the giving of gifts or personal praise, were received with an uncomfortable stillness, almost a complete silence. He had begun to sense his unimportance in the world, and any affection bestowed upon him only fueled these feelings of unworthiness. His parents had noticed this dramatic attitude change from the beginning, but they didn't think it was any cause for alarm.

They saw it as a phenomenon that accompanied adolescence, and therefore, it was also something that would pass, along with most of his other odd behavioral changes. But it was becoming more and more difficult to dismiss the sad behavior as a minor problem. Their hope had turned to worry, and their faith had all but been extinguished.

Mrs. Killingsworth's heart sank again as she noticed the fleeting look of sadness on Jeffrey's face. He was putting his left arm into one of the coat sleeves in a slow and reluctant manner while trying to hide the emotions he knew showed through his entire face. His mother was playing the same type of disguising act as she struggled to dam up the tears that were already forming in the corners of her eyes.

"Here, let me help you with that other sleeve," she said while shuffling to Jeffrey's right-hand side.

This gave her an excuse to move out of eye contact with him, and therefore, out of contact with the uncomfortable situation at hand. To the relief of them both, Mr. Killingsworth's footsteps could be heard leaving the kitchen and entering the hallway. The old wooden floor creaked beneath the weight of his tremendous stride. He was a tall man, well over six feet, with broad shoulders and a round chest.

His black hair and deeply set brown eyes, along with the overcoat that stretched all the way down to his knees, delivered somewhat of a forbidding appearance, but this was altogether contrary to his personality. He was the epitome of the friendly giant. As he wrapped one arm around his wife's shoulders and gently placed the other hand upon his son's head, it was evident that they loved their giant without constraint.

"That jacket looks sharp on you!" he declared in a cheerful voice and then began rubbing Jeffrey's head. "And the ten pairs of sweatpants don't look so bad, either," he added before bellowing a laugh that nearly shook the house off its foundation. "Are you ready to ride?"

"Yep, my bag's packed and everything," Jeffrey replied. "Lemme just take off a few pairs of these jogging pants, and I'll be set."

Jeffrey began stripping off the outer layers of sweatpants and flinging them left and right as if it were a way to eradicate the depressing thoughts that had been bugging him of late. When he looked up, his parents were pecking each other with soft kisses and giggling like children. His mother, standing on the very tips of her toes, resembled a child reaching to steal the stars from the sky.

She was short only in comparison to her husband's enormous height, but her small, slender frame helped to increase the notion that she was a tiny woman. Her dark, curly hair meandered halfway down her back like a softly flowing stream and was pinned up on the sides so that a few curls bounced gracefully around her dimpled cheeks.

The signs of middle age had begun to show in her face, first with slight wrinkles and then with unmistakable lines above her cheekbones and around her mouth, but the sparkle of vivacity that gleamed in her eyes seemed to suggest that she would not easily yield to the natural human process of creeping age and slow death.

As if waking from a dream, Jeffrey's parents stepped away from one another and confusedly began checking themselves for car keys, invitations, wallets, purses, and all the other objects necessary for their departure.

"All right, it looks like everything's in order," Mr. Killingsworth proclaimed as he performed the final pat-down on himself. "Jeffrey, go get William so we can tell him good-bye and grab your bag when you come back down."

Jeffrey covered half of the stairwell with only a few leaps and shouted his brother's name with an explosiveness that created an amusing crack in his voice. Within a few seconds, a young man of seventeen years rounded the banister and began descending the stairs. He looked shockingly similar to his father, as if they were carved from the same design. However, his eyes were a lighter shade of brown, causing them to be much less intense and intimidating. He was tall as well and had just recently grown into his long limbs. A great sense of pride emanated from his being and surrounded him on all sides.

"Y'all about to leave?" William asked as the silent excitement of having the house to himself shined beneath his dark countenance.

"Yes, we're heading out right now. Your mother and I may be back tonight if the weather permits. If not, then you'll have to pick up Jeffrey from the church around ten, and we'll see you both tomorrow. I'll leave your mother's keys right here on the hallway table and give you a call later to tell you when we're coming back."

Declarations of familial love and a round of sincere hugs were shared amongst the family before Jeffrey and his parents ventured out into the unsympathetic winter chill. They reached the car with ease, except for a few slips upon the iced-over sidewalk, and tumbled into the safety and warmth of the Mercedes parked out front.

Jeffrey pulled his right shirt sleeve down over his hand and began massaging the condensation off his window, but he could only clear a small portion before the dampness from the glass seeped through the thin cloth of his shirt. He was barely able to peer through the small, telescopic-like hole, but the view was enough to provide one final glimpse of his home before the car pulled out of the driveway.

Jeffrey's eyes began to pour over the house's elegant structure, and a calm smile formed upon his face. It was the only expression he could muster for the warmth and contentment that he felt, and he could only hope it was deserving of the only place he had ever called home. Jeffrey's "childhood sanctuary," as he liked to call it, was built in the Victorian stick style sometime in the late 1800s and had belonged to a long line of very successful entrepreneurs.

Made entirely of wood and possessing an air of the simpler times of the previous century, the house looked as if it would stand forever as proof that life had once contained a spirit of quiet pleasure, a spirit now lost to the speeding current of technology.

It stood two stories high, three including the attic, with a veranda on the first floor and a balcony hanging just above it. The paint was of a brown hue, closely resembling the natural color of the wood it covered, and the shutters were bloodred. In their younger years, Jeffrey and William had often imagined that the house was haunted.

Its age and overall creepy appearance, along with the constant creaking of the wooden floors, provided extra effects for their playful games. They would act as if they had seen terrible apparitions and try to describe them to one another. These games had gone on for quite some time, but William soon outgrew the childish adventurer within his heart, leaving Jeffrey to imagine alone.

At first this was upsetting, but in time Jeffrey learned to accept it, and consequently, he discovered that he didn't need any assistance in his playful endeavors. He could live and be entertained solely within his own mind. The focus of his daydreams turned from ghosts to the former inhabitants of the house.

He wondered what life was like for a person of wealth and high reputation at the turn of the twentieth century. His imagination originally carried him away to the formal dinner parties and occasional balls where the women discussed marriage prospects and the latest fashions while the men stood in corners smoking pipes and covering all the appropriate topics for educated gentlemen.

It all seemed so lively and entertaining to Jeffrey, but as time passed, his fantasies began to encompass the more solitary side of early twentieth-century life. He pictured lonely rooms dimly lit by a few candles where people sat quietly reading Milton or Dante, patiently waiting for either sleep or death. The house that had once exuded all the mystery and joys of the past now spoke of the quiet sorrows and the slow, sober lives it contained. And Jeffrey began to see that all the world and everything in it echoed the still, sad music of humanity.[1]

❧ 2 ❧

Jeffrey was suddenly awakened to reality by his father's passionate roars as he cursed random drivers on the busy interstate. He poked his head around the front passenger seat and began watching the cars dance from lane to lane, confidently testing and teasing the slick, snowy roads. Jeffrey could just begin to see the overwhelming change in the landscape and realized that he had been daydreaming for nearly the entire ride.

As the snow-capped mountains of Tennessee climbed triumphantly upon the horizon, his melancholy thoughts of the house and its lonely inhabitants faded into oblivion. A smile formed slowly upon his lips, and his eyes flickered at the thought of a day with his friends where the laughter and companionship would provide an escape from his own gloomy mindset.

"Jeffrey," Mrs. Killingsworth called as she maneuvered her body so her voice could carry to the back seat. "Is Natalie going to be there today?" She paused for a moment. After no response, she repeated her question in a more audible tone. "Is Natalie going to be there today?"

"Huh?" Jeffrey asked in a stupefied manner. "Sorry, I was thinking about something else. What did you ask me?"

"I asked you if Natalie was going with you all to Fall Creek today," Mrs. Killingsworth repeated.

"Oh…yeah," Jeffrey replied. "Well, I think so."

Natalie Spellman was just a few months away from her fourteenth birthday, but her stature made her look like she was approaching her twelfth. She possessed very tiny hands and feet along with a petite figure, which created the image that she was of a delicate and fragile nature. The tips of her black, silky hair barely rested upon her narrow shoulders, and her calm, aqua-colored eyes appeared peaceful, like clear, tropical waters. Her smile alone was attractive, but when accompanied by the often-insecure look in her eyes, it was exceptionally stunning.

She and Jeffrey had grown up down the street from each other and had been friends long before either of them could remember, but the last year and a half had witnessed the creation of a gulf between them. The emotional changes they were both experiencing turned their relaxed childhood relationship into one composed of awkward silences and constant stuttering and stammering, mainly on the part of Jeffrey.

He contemplated this dilemma until his brain ran wild, but he could never figure out what made him so nervous. One day it would be a playful wink, the next an innocent touch on the shoulder, but they all had the same effect. He had never dreamed that his behavior could waver so much on account of such minute actions from a girl. Natalie was his first boyhood crush.

"She is such a pretty girl and is always so polite," Mrs. Killingsworth said. "You should ask her to go to the movies sometime."

"We've been to the movies before, a lot of times," Jeffrey replied while continuously staring out the rear window.

"Yes, I know that, but it's different now," his mother returned. "You know what I mean."

"Yeah, I know," Jeffrey rejoined. "I'll ask her sometime...just not right now."

The car rolled to a stop beside two expensive SUVs and a raggedy-looking van with *Sunnyside Baptist Church* written on the side. It appeared that everyone had just arrived because many of them were still stretching their legs as a result of being cramped in a car for so long.

"Good, I'm not late," Jeffrey proclaimed with a breath of relief.

He then began twisting and contorting his body to the left, then to the right, in a tiresome attempt to put his coat on in the back seat. When he reached for his bag, he looked up to see his parents smiling at him.

"I love y'all too," Jeffrey said before jumping out of the car and rushing to join his friends.

As he approached the van, Natalie was the first to catch his eye. She was wearing a firm-fitting wool sweater and black spandex tights, an outfit that inspired Jeffrey's hormones to rush through him like wild horses. His attempt to avoid staring at her curvature was a futile effort, but luckily, she was just turning around when he began to retract his gaze. She waved at him in a silly fashion, like she used to do when they were kids, and smiled cheerfully before turning back around to face the boy standing near her.

His name was Johnny Greersby. He and Natalie had been talking for a few months and had just recently given their relationship the proficient title of "going steady." All of a sudden, Natalie became the envy of every girl in school. The drastically important telephone and locker room conversations, which had formerly revolved around Johnny's baby blue eyes and effeminately soft blond hair, now turned into a chaotic array of disbelief over how Natalie had nabbed the best-looking guy in school.

Johnny was certainly not in the dark about any of the current hoopla. It gratified him to the utmost degree and served to boost his already overblown confidence. Consequently, he developed a new strut, put a little more smoothness into his voice, and paraded around like nothing could touch him. However, he couldn't help but envy Jeffrey's history with Natalie. Whenever he was around, Johnny's arrogance would give way to feelings of insecurity, and his smile would twist into a scowl, ruining his boyish charm altogether.

Upon noticing the familiar grimace on Johnny's countenance, Jeffrey returned his look with a sincere, yet timid wave and then bent his steps toward a more welcoming party.

"Hey, Jimmy! What's up, Mark?" Jeffrey proclaimed with an almost forced enthusiasm.

"Hey, man!" they both hollered in unison before nearly jerking his arms out of socket with the usual shaking and slapping of hands.

"What's up with Johnny and Natalie huddled up in the corner over there?" Jeffrey muttered as he peeped over his shoulder to catch one more glimpse of the sickening sight.

"I don't know what's wrong with 'em, man," Jimmy uttered as he slowly shook his head from side to side. "I guess they're true lovin' too much to talk with anybody else. I wouldn't worry about it if I were you. It's way too nice of a day to be stressin' over some girl. Sure, it's cold as heck!" Jimmy proclaimed as his shivering hand reached out to give Jeffrey a somewhat comforting slap on the back. "But it's still a nice day."

Jimmy Weathers was a handsome boy of dark-brown complexion. He viewed his good looks as a huge commodity for getting girls and convincing others of his good nature. However, his new-found height gave him a somewhat awkward appearance, as if he was still getting used to the tremendous changes from childhood to young adulthood.

He often clumsily stumbled around with little notice or alarm and constantly ran into things and other people. With all this, though, he still carried himself with supreme confidence, as if the world was licking from the trough at his feet.

"Hey, Jeffrey boy, real quick, my teeth look clean?" Jimmy suddenly asked.

"Yeah, they're all right," Jeffrey said nonchalantly while continuing to look over his shoulder.

Jimmy could already see it would take some effort to get his best friend out of the pits and onto solid ground for the day. If he couldn't succeed, he figured he would just have to bear it out with him. It wouldn't be any big deal—just another instance of Jimmy's sincere devotion to his friends.

Though it was uncommon to witness this type of benevolence among adolescents, it was not without good reason. Jimmy had grown up as an only child to parents who were committed to their professions more than anything else. Though his house was filled with wealth, it was entirely void of affection.

While the other children in the neighborhood dreamed of new remote-controlled cars or shiny, sleek bicycles, Jimmy only wished for a friend with whom he could share his thoughts and possessions. In the process, he learned that a good friend was pretty hard to come by. And seeing Jeffrey now in such a disheartening situation, Jimmy concocted a plan that was sure to turn his mind toward more cheerful things. After all, anything that involved clowning around in order to distract others was right up his alley.

"Hey, Mark, show Jeffrey that joint you brought with you," Jimmy said while looking around to make sure their youth minister was not around.

"Check it out," Mark whispered as he slyly pulled the joint out of his jacket pocket and began showing it to the two of them. "I found it in that crazy-lookin' box in my brother's room—the one with the peace signs and the purple mushrooms. Anyway, if we get a chance to sneak off for a little while, we'll see if it's any good."

Mark Jerkins was considered the "bad boy" of the neighborhood. It wasn't that he was any worse than the other kids; he just wasn't as discreet about his behavior as they were. Nevertheless, all the local parents worked very hard at keeping their beloved children away from him. Mark's ruddy appearance didn't help the matter much, either.

He was underdressed for every occasion, showing up in worn-out blue jeans or a hole-covered T-shirt emblazoned with obvious drug or alcohol paraphernalia. He also possessed a sneaky smile that seemed to mock any authority figure bold enough to come into its presence.

Perhaps this bad reputation, which bloomed from such superficialities as these, was formed by the locals a little prematurely, but this was the way opinions had been formed for years, and they saw no need to change now. The scrutinizing eye of the public had, in fact, been on the entire Williams family long before Mark could even spell the words "white trash."

Now, with one child in the midst of a nasty drug habit and the other well on the way, dislike slowly rolled into disdain for the parents who were unable to provide their children with the proper guidance they so desperately needed. This unreasonable viewpoint was more or less held by the entire community, but it especially rested in the eyes and minds of fellow parents who knew their kids had been raised too well to succumb to such a social embarrassment as drug addiction.

"I can't believe you brought weed on a church trip! You know, you may be crazy, but you may also be a genius," Jeffrey uttered as he returned Mark's sly smile with one of his own. "If nothing else, Brother Rodney's famous char-blackened hamburgers might taste good after we smoke."

The three boys doubled over with laughter and began slapping their knees like moonshine-delirious hillbillies until they were suddenly startled by Brother Rodney's deafening voice. They wheeled around quickly, fearing that he had overheard their conversation, but their worries were quickly put to rest when they realized his purpose for yelling was to summon the group.

"Bring it in, everyone! Bring it in!" he shouted in a tone similar to that of a football coach toward his players after a well-executed practice.

Yelling in this fashion was a habit of Brother Rodney's that would die as grudgingly as his football career had done. Perhaps it was his only way of reenacting the glory days in which the smell of sour grass on his worn-out pair of cleats signified a sweet aroma and the thumping of the band on a stadium-lit Friday night swayed in harmony with the butterflies in his stomach. Those days had expired much too early for Brother Rodney.

His hopes of playing in college came to a grinding halt when he nearly broke his neck trying to serve a knockout tackle during a heated backyard football game. The doctors said the damage wasn't extensive enough to cause paralysis or warrant surgery, but it was sufficient to deem a career in football much too dangerous to attempt.

Therefore, Brother Rodney decided to enter seminary instead of attending a four-year college that he couldn't afford. After several painstaking years of quarreling with God, he accepted his lot as a mere servant and became a youth minister in the famous mining town of Dahlonega, Georgia.

Now he stood before this group of adolescents, a man thirty-five years young who seemed to have aged as quickly as his football career had ended. His jet-black hair that was once so full and wavy now stretched in desperation atop his slightly balding head, and his eyes, a watery blue, revealed no indication of the ferocity they had once contained. He looked physically beaten, as if he were simply going through the motions, waiting for the grave to swallow his misery.

Yet in Brother Rodney's case, looks were very deceiving. He was, in reality, happier now than he had ever been on the field of fame and physical conquest. For the first time in his life, he possessed the only thing that ever really mattered, the only thing he could not bear to lose—a peaceful soul.

"All right! Is this everyone?" Brother Rodney exclaimed as he perused the group in front of him.

"No, Molly and Madison aren't here yet," Jimmy replied. "I think they were ridin' together."

"Well, they'll be here soon enough," Brother Rodney rejoined as he examined the cheap plastic watch on his wrist. "In the meantime, let's go over the plans for the day. Cooking will begin promptly at twelve o'clock, so we need to get the coals going within the next few minutes. Guys, grab the food, charcoal, and metal pans in the back of the van, please, and follow me over to the far-right cabin in the row. There's not enough for each of you to carry, so decide amongst yourselves. Natalie, you can walk with me if you'd like."

Mark was the first to enter the van and begin the assembly-line process of removing all the pans. The reason for this was evident once the van door was shut and all the boys were standing outside again: Jimmy with a bag of charcoal and a canister of lighter fluid; Jeffrey with hot dogs, ground beef, and buns; Johnny with cooking utensils, condiments, and plates; and Mark with nothing but a sly smile that stretched from ear to ear.

"How come you don't have to carry anything?" Johnny asked with obvious frustration.

"'Cause I'm supervisin'," Mark replied while chuckling to himself. "Now, let's move it, Johnny Boy."

The four boys began to descend the snowy hill toward the cabin, all the while aggravating one another with various childish games. Jimmy was swinging the bag of charcoal into Jeffrey's back while Jeffrey attempted to trip Mark by kicking one foot into the other. Johnny was yanking off each of their toboggans and slamming them to the ground. Suffice it to say, by the bottom of the hill the four stooges were lucky to have gotten themselves and the supplies there in one piece.

$$\Longleftarrow 3 \Longrightarrow$$

The cabin was positioned on a gently sloping hill, nestled between a semi-frozen stream and an endless display of enormously haunting pine trees. At its farthest end, the hill dropped off into a freefall exhibition of telephone poles, slanting trees, and beautiful white snow, all desperately clinging to their feeble grip upon the mountainside.

Along some of the more jagged points, numerous houses sat teetering on the edge of destruction while the inhabitants calmly drank hot cocoa and cider, waiting for the ski lifts to open. A little lower down, the mountain became alive with people weaving in and out of streets and stores, oblivious to those watching them from far greater heights.

"Isn't this view awe-inspiring?" Brother Rodney exclaimed with a wide look of wonder in his eyes. "I can never see something like this without thinking…how can people not believe in God?"

"I see your point exactly," Mark replied. "Isn't the evidence overwhelming?"

"Yes, it truly is," rejoined Brother Rodney. He nodded his head very slowly, then closed his eyes for a few seconds as if trying to trap that image within his mind for all of eternity. Then, turning toward the boys with the same radiating smile that Moses brought down from Mount Sinai, Brother Rodney said, "However, we've got bigger fish to fry right now, or should I say burgers and dogs to grill."

He chuckled to himself as he picked up the bag of charcoal. "Y'all don't know nothin' about this Southern-style grillin'. Check it out!" Brother Rodney nearly dumped the charcoal on the ground before realizing the bag had a split down the side of it. "Ooooh, close call. Maybe I bragged a little too soon," he humorously proclaimed before maneuvering the charcoal into some sort of an awkward pyramid.

"Now we're ready," Brother Rodney said while nodding his head with infinite satisfaction. "Can you hand me that lighter fluid, Jimmy?" Brother Rodney dashed the fluid horizontally, vertically, and finally in circles. Once the coals appeared to be saturated, he closed the grill and said, "That's all we can do for the time being. Let's go check this cabin out. I believe Natalie's already inside. Oh, Jimmy, Jeffrey, grab those containers with the meat and plates, please."

They all entered the cabin, Jimmy and Jeffrey bringing up the rear with another showcase of professional horseplay as they attempted to put the freezing metal trays up against each other's necks.

"Wow, this is cool!" Johnny shouted as he gazed wide-eyed across the room. "Check out all the dead animals on the walls and the old cast-iron fireplace in the corner. Did people really use those, Brother Rodney?"

"Yep, back in the old days, when the folks used to rough it up here in the woods. We may try to fire the ol' timer up if it gets cold enough."

"Then I hope it gets colder!" Johnny responded with unbridled enthusiasm. "Natalie, don't you think this cabin is awesome?"

Natalie had been fixating on the stuffed head of a grizzly bear for the past few minutes. She suddenly broke her stare and turned toward Johnny.

"Yeah, it's okay, I guess."

The cabin was, in fact, less than impressive. Its construction more closely resembled a grouping of preassembled logs from a toy set than it did an original feat of sweat and ingenuity. In addition, some of the animals that silently decorated the walls weren't even native to the region. Yet somehow amidst all the artificiality, the cabin retained some small quality of familiarity and charm. Then again, one can always gain a warm, homely sort of feeling from log walls and wooden floors no matter how phony the scenery may be.

Jimmy and Jeffrey had been wandering from one stuffed head to the next, poking and prodding at the eyes and making silly jokes. All the while, Jeffrey was very careful to avoid Natalie, who was now arm in arm with her beloved boyfriend by the fireplace. Suddenly, Jimmy pointed toward the next head on the wall and whispered to Jeffrey, "Hey, man, what would you do if you looked up and that moose was smokin' a blunt?"

The two boys went into hysterics, Jeffrey intentionally laughing the harder so Natalie could hear how good of a time he was having. When the amusement finally died out, they ventured over to the opposite side of the room, where Mark and Brother Rodney were seasoning the meat and mashing it into patties.

"What y'all doin'?" Jeffrey asked while striving to gain a look over one of their shoulders.

"Gettin' the meat ready for the grill," Brother Rodney replied. "I've got Mark helpin' me here. Gonna teach him how to grill the old-school way. Since y'all aren't doing anything, wouldya' mind lighting those coals for me?"

"No problem," Jimmy responded.

"Oh, and be careful not to stand too close when you fire it up. The flames may be a little jumpy at first."

"That's cool. Is the lighter fluid still outside, Brother Rodney?"

"Yeah, I believe so, but you probably won't need to add any more on. Why do you ask?"

"No reason." Jimmy gave Jeffrey a mischievous glance, nudged him in the rib cage, and the two clowns pimp-walked their way out of the cabin.

"What are you gonna do, juice it with lighter fluid?" Jeffrey asked as they stepped outside into the wintry air.

"Heck, yeah! We're gonna turn that grill into a bonfire!"

With that said, Jimmy tore off a small piece of the charcoal bag, lit it, and threw it into the grill. When the coals burst into flames, he began to sing, "Burn, baby, burn! Disco inferno! Burn, baby, burn!" Once the fire had died down to some degree, Jimmy shot it with a heavy dose of lighter fluid. It immediately exploded like a violent revolution and then sluggishly returned to its boring, sober state, at which time Jimmy raised his singing voice to a booming level and summoned the flames again.

As Jeffrey stared into the dancing inferno, a dark cloud took form within his mind. He began to lose focus, and suddenly, his cheerful mood floated away like the smoke from the fire. He knew that within an instant, a pyroclastic surge of anxiety and sorrow would rush through him, cruelly twisting his perception until the very notion of happiness seemed ridiculous. *Why is this happening?* Jeffrey wondered as he clenched his teeth and strained his eyes.

A feeling of panic rocked his soul. He tried to think of something uplifting, but his scattered thoughts always seemed to drift back to Natalie in some roundabout way. He couldn't help but picture her face alongside his happiest moments, but now, with her attention directed so much toward another, those moments were poisoned. Still, in the spirit of self-torture, he found himself once again dwelling upon the most embittered memory of all. It had occurred at a time when Jeffrey was first experiencing the tremendous need for acceptance and the eccentricity of sexual attraction.

On Natalie's twelfth birthday, her mother had arranged for a huge party to be thrown in their backyard. Everyone was expected to dress a little more formal than usual, but most of the kids didn't even know what "formal" meant. When they found out they had to wear church clothes to a birthday party, they flew into an outrage.

Without a doubt, Natalie was the angriest of all. She had always been accustomed to dressing like a tomboy when she and her friends went out to explore the woods or ride bikes around the neighborhood, but on that day, her mother had declared with the pounding of her gavel that she must dress like a lady.

Natalie was nearly the last one to join the party when she glided across the backyard wearing a yellow sundress that extended just above her knees. Her hair was uniformly flowing downward except for two braids that circled around her head and connected in the back. She blushed a little under Jeffrey's stare and slightly tilted her head downward in embarrassment as she approached him.

If he had looked away right then, he could have escaped untouched, but he continued to gaze at this new and wonderful creature he had seen so many times and yet had never seen before. Then she began to smile, and the loveliness that played upon her face totally engulfed him. At that moment, he knew with both dread and joy that he would never look at her quite the same again.

Now the vivid recollection of her timid eyes and bashful smile created the sensation that she was almost within his grasp, but the reality of his miserable situation abruptly surfaced, ravaging Jeffrey's already declining fortitude. His immediate, unconscious reaction was to block it all out, to turn his attention back to the real world at hand and the blazing inferno that demoniacally hovered before his eyes.

"You alright?" Jimmy asked with a quality of both concern and curiosity.

"Yeah, I'm fine."

"You sure? I thought I'd lost you there for a minute."

"I guess I'm back now. Hand me that lighter fluid."

"Okay, but you have to sing. You can't get into it without the 'burn, baby, burn.'"

Jeffrey and Jimmy began wailing like a chorus of crazed dogs until suddenly, the sound of footsteps crunching in the snow interrupted their playful experiment.

"You guys are so immature," Madison snobbishly pronounced when the two boys turned around.

"Yep, and proud of it!" Jimmy proclaimed with a tone of indignation. "Y'all are a little late, aren't you?"

"Yes," Molly replied in a soft voice before giving Jimmy a warm hug around the neck. "We were waiting on Madison to get ready."

People were always waiting on Madison in some form or another. She was from one of the wealthiest and most influential families in Dahlonega—the Willinghams. Therefore, it was common courtesy for people to place her upon a pedestal as if she was actually made of gold. For those wrapped up in the superficial side of life, the envy did not end with her prominence—Madison was gorgeous, as well.

Her high cheekbones and defined jawline produced an unmatched appearance of balance and symmetry. In addition, she possessed a head of naturally blond hair that was never out of place and a set of large blue eyes that were nothing short of spectacular.

Unfortunately, Madison's vanity was the only thing that exceeded her beauty and inheritance. She craved the adoration of others so much that her self-image had grown to include the flashing of camera bulbs and the praises of the lowly as they groveled at her feet.

The mink coat, flashy jewelry, and red carpet served as special effects within these delusions of grandeur. From the very start, Madison was one for whom the world performed, and so it was no great surprise for her to turn and embrace it (along with its materialistic splendor) with an equal passion.

Molly Corbin, on the other hand, had nothing to be vain about. She came from a relatively poor family and had none of the charming physical characteristics that Madison constantly boasted of, yet despite their differences, they managed to get along just fine. Molly always enjoyed the enchanting atmosphere that accompanied Madison's presence, and Madison equally enjoyed Molly looking so out of place in the luxurious environment only she could provide.

Madison had often tried to dress her in a more elegant style but had failed miserably each time, and for good measure. Molly was not attractive in a glamorous way. Her beauty, which was firmly constrained within the normal, everyday sense, made her the type of girl one would expect to see at a local ice-cream stand rather than within the lonely-hearted dreams of a young man.

She had frizzy blond hair that decorated her head like

strings of cotton candy and eyes that first appeared blue but were really a unique concoction of light browns and dull greens. Her best trait was her cute, chubby cheeks. They would inflate around her tiny mouth when she smiled or laughed, and suddenly her appearance would become as pleasant as a child's.

Molly had a wonderful sense of humor as well, which is why her relationship with Jimmy was such a playful one. They teased one another constantly, showing neither sensitivity nor constraint, except when they were immersed in one another's kisses or rolling around like sex-starved lunatics. It was during these times that he valued her skin 'n' bones figure and she his cute, mouse-like ears.

Otherwise, both these qualities were fair play for a number of jokes, as was anything or anyone else within their sight. Jeffrey discovered this tendency of theirs—to make jokes out of everything—the hard way, or rather the embarrassing way, about a year previously.

He had not long been acquainted with Molly and Jimmy when he gained firsthand experience of the humiliation they could produce. It just so happened that the bus for school was running early one morning when Jeffrey rushed out of the house, only to hear the engine rumbling toward its next destination. His father, who was driving a rusty-red 1962 Ford pickup at the time, offered to give him a ride on his way to work.

Jeffrey consented, and after lingering around for ten minutes or so, they left en route to Highland Middle School. When they arrived, much to Jeffrey's dismay, the buses had just begun unloading passengers. *Aw, man,* Jeffrey thought as he attempted to scurry away from the truck before being spotted by his friends.

Suddenly, he heard Molly humming the tune to "Sanford and Son" loud enough for everyone around to hear. Jeffrey turned around slowly, hoping his face wasn't as red as it felt, when Jimmy approached him, nearly laughing too hard to walk. He slapped Jeffrey on the shoulder and proclaimed, "Aww, don't be sore. If it makes you feel any better, you can give me one across the lips, like Fred Sanford used to say." Then he began to laugh again and almost dropped his books all over the ground.

Ultimately, Jeffrey could see the humor in the situation, that is, once his embarrassment abated, but it was duly noted that in the future he would avoid any potentially humiliating situations when Molly and Jimmy were around to announce them to the world.

"Hello, Jeffrey," Molly cheerfully shouted before giving him a playful, yet somewhat powerful, punch in the arm.

"You know, you sure have a talent for greeting people," Jeffrey said while massaging the soreness out of his shoulder. "They should give you one of those jobs at Walmart so you can stand at the front entrance and punch everyone in the arm as they come in the door."

He looked over to see if Madison might crack a smile, but if he thought she actually would, he was sorely mistaken. She tightened her brow to deliver her most serious look, a definite sign that she was putting on airs, and then she exclaimed, "It's cold out here. I'm going inside."

"Good idea, mademoiselle," Jimmy quickly retorted.

Then, acting as if he were carrying the tails of her imaginary gown, Jimmy followed closely behind like a belittled servant. When Madison reached the cabin door, Jimmy turned to Jeffrey and Molly and gave the sign that the other servants were to follow. The three of them cracked up laughing as they staggered into the cabin's warm and caring walls.

≈4≈

The air within the cabin was thick with tension. Madison elegantly held the stage with a dinner party-like conversation on why her outfit was so fitting for the occasion, whereas Natalie's contained too much blue and purple lining for this time of year. It was Madison's opening act, and as she spoke, she exhibited a grace that was rarely seen in an age when kings and queens had been demoted to the likes of normal people.

She was a Cleopatra in a room full of peasants and paupers. However, most of the group knew her well enough by now to see the fraud in the formality. It was expected, commonplace, and therefore more humorous than offensive.

"Hey, ask her how many people you're supposed to invite to a party if the summer solstice is in effect, and um, Mars and Venus are lined up with the moon," Jimmy whispered to Jeffrey, desperately trying not to explode in laughter.

Upon overhearing the comment and seeing the two of them with watery eyes and choking throats, Brother Rodney swallowed his own laugh and gave them a look that suggested better decorum and politeness toward Madison. Once he had regained control of his voice, Brother Rodney politely interrupted her in order to inform the group of the plans for the afternoon.

"All right, everyone. It's time to cook. It should take, say, twenty to thirty minutes for everything to be ready. So, you can stay in the cabin or go walking in the woods or just wander around the campsite if you'd like. Just be careful, whatever you do, and don't get too close to the edge of the mountainside."

Brother Rodney picked up the tray and walked out of the cabin. Jeffrey was the first to follow, knowing that another two seconds within those tight, closed walls would surely suffocate him. Natalie and Johnny trailed close behind, arm in arm and stride for stride, like the winners of a three-legged race. Molly came next, humming a tune and bouncing her curly hair to some imaginary beat that she alone could hear. Mark and Jimmy were the last to leave. They shot out of that pressure cooker wearing anxious smiles, a sure sign that their chance for delinquency had arrived.

"You ready to smoke?" Jimmy asked rhetorically.

"Oh, yeah!" Mark responded while fidgeting his hands in his pockets. "Hang on one second," he said as he turned back toward the cabin. "Madison, you comin' outside with everyone?"

"No, I think I'll stay in here where it's warm and cozy," she answered with a dejected air.

"What, you worried about Madison now?" Jimmy said with a grin, as if he had just solved some elaborate mystery.

"No, it's nothing like that. I was just curious. So, we gonna take a walk in the woods?"

Jimmy decided to let the serious subject drop in order to focus on the more enjoyable, and therefore, more important issue at hand.

"Yep. Let's holler at Jeffrey real quick."

There was really no need. Jeffrey was already walking toward them and motioning his hands like he was flagging down a cab.

"Hey, I've already told Brother Rodney that we're going exploring in the woods," Jeffrey said. "Are y'all ready?"

"Yeah," Jimmy replied before motioning to Molly that she should come with them.

"No thanks," Molly responded. "I haven't gotten to talk to Natalie yet, so I'll probably just stay here. Y'all have fun, though."

Jimmy blew her a kiss, an attempt to be funny more than sweet, then caught up with Jeffrey and Mark at the edge of the woods. Anxious to distance themselves from the group, they plunged into the snow with rapid feet and pounding hearts, but their burning lungs soon convinced them to slacken their pace a little. Their supposed easy hike through barren trees and drifts of snow had quickly become akin to a journey by elephant through the Alps. The snow was piled so heavily upon the ground that the earth groaned beneath its tremendous weight.

Consequently, every step for the boys was more difficult than the last, like the transition into old age where the joints grow stiff, and the muscles take early leave. Even the wind, howling at them through icicled branches and snow cone-cold air, seemed to oppose their experimental clash with nature. Yet the three discoverers reluctantly pushed on and eventually reached their ultimate destination, where prying eyes failed to penetrate the depth and obscurity of the shivering forest.

"You think this is far enough?" Mark asked in a faint, struggling voice.

"It'd better be! I think we just climbed half the mountain," Jeffrey responded with his hands on his knees and his lungs in his throat.

"Yeah, I think we're good," Jimmy claimed as he unsuccessfully peered through the vortex of airborne snow and arthritic tree limbs. "Go ahead and fire it up!"

After struggling for a moment to fish the joint out of his pocket, Mark slowly raised the precious jewel toward his mouth, pausing briefly to admire its streamline quality.

"Hey, we may need to block this wind, or we'll never get it lit," he said while motioning to Jeffrey and Jimmy to move in around him.

The lighter sparked several times but to no avail. Whenever the flame emerged, it was quickly snuffed out by the domineering wind.

"Y'all, raise your jackets off your shoulders a little," Mark said before striking the lighter again.

On the seventh try, the three-man-barricade strategy finally worked, and the joint came to life, glowing like a beacon of light for weary travelers who had lost their way. Mark could hear the weed crackle and pop as the smoke whistled through the thin paper. After a few tokes, his lungs were content. He held his breath, waiting for the tetrahydrocannabinol (THC) to embrace his bloodstream, then exhaled the thick smoke in a sigh of relief.

"Man, this is some good stuff," he said in a low, muffled voice before passing the joint in Jeffrey's direction.

Jeffrey grabbed the joint with eager hands and began pulling on it as if gasping for air. The smoke raced into his lungs, perhaps a little too quickly, and Jeffrey started coughing and hacking like his insides were coming out, lungs first. Jimmy, who had been standing there with his hand out, anxiously waiting like the last leg on a relay team, was finally able to catch Jeffrey in between coughs.

He laughed at Jeffrey for his smoking inexperience as he took the joint with his forefinger and thumb. Then he puffed on it in short, successive spurts, pausing briefly between intervals to let a little smoke creep out of his wind-chapped lips.

Before long, the three of them were hazy-eyed and laughing. Most of the ensuing conversation consisted of silly, rambling stories or jokes that were downright jive, but it didn't seem to matter. They were caught up in that perfect mixture of paranoia and euphoria, unable and unwilling to suppress the scatterbrained thoughts that fed their delirious behavior. Their usual inhibitions rested comfortably in oblivion, but they could not continue to disregard the bitter wind that gnawed at their exposed flesh.

"It's gettin' a little nippy out here, ain't it!" Mark exclaimed while hugging himself and bouncing up and down.

"Yeah, it is!" Jimmy earnestly replied.

"So, y'all about ready to go back to the campsite?" Mark returned.

"I'm way too high to be around all those other people right now," Jeffrey joined in. "But y'all can go ahead."

"What, and leave you out here by yourself?" Jimmy responded. "Yeah, that would be real smart," he commented sarcastically before turning to Mark. "Hey, I'll stay here with him until he regains his composure."

"Okay," Mark replied. "Build a snowman for me while you're out here." He turned and began trudging through the snow before yelling, "I'll see y'all in a little while. You can find me beside the hamburgers."

Mark was out of sight within several seconds. The snow was falling heavier now, and it was becoming difficult to see even ten yards away. Jimmy and Jeffrey looked in amazement at the cluster of snowflakes that fluttered in the air. They seemed to dance chaotically, torn between one way and another as if stunned by the prospect of limitless possibility.

But then the cold breeze rushed through, gathering them by the thousands and swirling them together like a flock of birds. Only then did they look content—driven by a free wind, pushing upward into the sky as if aspiring to greatness, then recklessly speeding toward the earth and their own impending destruction.

"Check it out!" Jeffrey exclaimed while tilting his head back and sticking out his tongue so he could catch the snowflakes in his mouth. "See, it's not that bad out here. It may even start to warm up." He laughed as soon as the words left his mouth, then looked at Jimmy with squinting, bloodshot eyes.

"Yeah, I bet," Jimmy said before knocking Jeffrey off balance with a playful shove. "Come on. Maybe if we walk, it won't be so cold."

"All right. There's a creek up here I wanna check out anyway. I wonder if it's frozen over yet."

"You mean the one just over this hill?" Jimmy pointed toward the gradual incline just slightly to their left.

"No, I think it's this way," Jeffrey said while motioning toward his right.

"You sure? I'm almost positive it's right over that hill. Oh well, it doesn't matter. We'll go your way first. If it's not right, we can always circle back around."

"Sounds good." Jeffrey began high-stepping through the thick snow. "Did you watch the Green Bay game last Sunday?"

The words were lost on Jimmy. He had already tightened up the strings on his hood and ducked his head down to avoid the ear-numbing wind. Throughout the walk, he hardly looked up except to see how far Jeffrey was in front of him. He simply followed his tracks, stepping exactly where Jeffrey had stepped in the attempt to conserve some of his own energy.

Those tracks eventually led him atop a hill that looked down into a valley where the snow was smoothly and evenly laid out like an antique rug on a hard, wooden floor. Amidst the scattered pines that populated the icy runway, there were a few old, broken-down cabins, but not a creek in sight.

"I guess you may have been right, Jimmy," Jeffrey said nonchalantly.

"Yeah, I know, but it's all right. It's still kind of a nice sight, the cabins and all." Jimmy rested his hands upon his knees as he peered out over the landscape. "You wanna rest for a minute?"

"Yeah, that's cool." Jeffrey started to smile, and his eyes developed an inquiring look. "Hey, do you think hillbillies might live in those cabins?"

"Shoot, I don't even know if hillbillies still exist."

"Yeah, but if they did, do you think they might live in those cabins?"

"Man, all I know is, if I see some inbred with no teeth come out of one of those shacks, I'm runnin'!" Their laughter was exemplified by the condensation that exploded from their winded lungs.

"Man, stop!" Jeffrey exclaimed. "I can hardly breathe." He took a few deep breaths of air and composed himself. "Whew, that was funny. Hey, how come you never hear about black hillbillies? I mean, aren't they always white?"

"Man, you think of some of the craziest stuff," Jimmy replied. "I would've never thought something like that in a million years." Jimmy knelt and placed his hand under his chin as if to imitate the thinking man statue. "All right, see if you can stay with me on this one. There may be something in this theory I have that applies to this hillbilly situation. It recently occurred to me that black people and white people handle their problems very differently.

"Now, black people have been oppressed a lot in their history," Jimmy continued, "but they always seemed to handle it so well. I've always wondered how, but now I think I get it. It comes down to patience. No matter what the hardship is, we always handle it with grace. Grace and patience, that's what it's about. Maybe we've learned it in time, or maybe it's in our genes or something, I don't know for sure, but it's definitely there."

"Grace and patience," Jeffrey repeated. "Yeah, I like that, but I have no idea where you're going with this."

"Hold your horses. I'm gettin' to it. Now, white people are just crazy. When real hard times strike, they totally lose it. Some have nervous breakdowns. Some pull out a rifle and start shooting people. You see, these hillbillies up here are handling their misfortunes in a productive way. Instead of wreaking havoc, they drink their moonshine and yell at the trees. Does that make any sense?"

"I don't know, man. If I think about it with what you call the 'crazy' part of my brain, then it does. All right, well, let me ask you this. What about the people who don't take off for the woods because of something bad that happened, the people who just seem to do it for no reason?"

"Aw, that's because of the government," Jimmy spurted out while trying not to laugh. "You hear 'em, don't you? Listen out there in the woods. The government, the government got me… soundin' like some schizophrenic or something."

"That's funny," Jeffrey responded as he pictured a dirty, rough-looking man wearing a long beard and cut-off fatigues. "I think you've got something there, Jimmy." He paused for a second to sort out the strange, yet seemingly important information, then suddenly said, "What in the world are we talkin' about?"

"Beats me. Nothing worth relating to anyone else." Jimmy just shook his head, smiled, and pulled his hood up again. "You ready to walk?"

"Yeah, sure. You lead the way this time."

Jimmy took one last look at the cabins and cringed at the thought of the strange activities that must have taken place in them. The chill down his spine was enough to send him rushing down the hill in a most careless manner. When he reached the bottom, he was amazed that he hadn't fallen and broken his leg, but even more amazing was the fact that it had stopped snowing.

He pulled off his hood and peeked up at the sky in disbelief just as the sun emerged from the clouds and spewed radiation upon the refrigerated earth. With the warmth from the sun striking his face, Jimmy was no longer thinking of creepy cabins and strange mountain men. He had even forgotten about Jeffrey until, suddenly, a snowball came crashing into the back of his head.

"Why'd you take off like that?" Jeffrey yelled with obvious frustration.

"Oh, I thought I saw that hunchback guy that's always in those horror movies. What's his name?"

"Who? Igor?"

"Yeah! Igor! He was standing on the front porch of one of those shacks. I think he had a broom in his hands."

"Man, stop. You know you didn't see no Igor."

Jimmy knew Jeffrey was a little perturbed, but he couldn't help smiling a little at the absurdity of his Igor story. Jeffrey didn't notice. He was looking up at the sky, wondering where the snow had gone. When he finally looked back down, Jimmy was chuckling and smiling from ear to ear like the fair just rode into town.

"You're a trip, man," Jeffrey said. "All right, this time we're gonna walk side by side. We can take our time now since it's not so cold."

"Cool." Jimmy was silent for a moment while he wiped the remaining part of the snowball off his neck. Then, he turned toward Jeffrey with a look of terror and said "Naw, for real, you didn't see him?"

"Who?" Jeffrey asked.

"Igor! He shuffled out on the porch like this." Jimmy hunched over and held one hand on the small of his back. With the other, he pretended to carry a broom while he slowly limped toward Jeffrey. The look of terror on his face grew even more intense, then he continued, "Check it out! All of a sudden, this creepy smile formed on his face, right.

"I thought he was about to look right at me," Jimmy said, "but instead he turned toward the cabin door. Then, in this raspy, evil-sounding voice, he said, 'Yes, master, we've done it, the porch is clean.' Once he started doing one of those evil, 'I just took over the world' type of laughs, I got the heck out of there."

"Man, you're crazy," Jeffrey burst out as he nearly fell in the snow laughing. "Where do you come up with this stuff?"

"Aw, that ain't nothin'. Check it out. Here goes my impression of Dracula cleanin' off people's windshields like the homeless do, only he uses bloody rags instead of newspapers."

In between Jimmy's antics and Jeffrey's tendency to fall down laughing every two seconds, it was a miracle they ever made it back to the other side, where they planned to find the creek. The temperature had increased at least five degrees, and it almost felt nice outside. Jimmy and Jeffrey simultaneously shed their coats and gazed out over the lonely, incandescent tundra.

When no creek presented itself, they squinted their eyes and searched farther into the distance. With hands just above their brows and heads pivoting from side to side, they looked like a modern-day Lewis and Clark. Unfortunately, the resemblance applied only to appearance.

"Dang it, man!" Jeffrey said suddenly. "They must have moved that creek since last year."

"Either that or we're lost," Jimmy replied while snickering under his breath. "But I think I like your theory better."

"So, what do you wanna do?" Jeffrey returned.

"Doesn't matter to me. You still high?"

"Yeah. I think I'm starting to come down, though."

"All right, let's go back to the campsite, then. I'm gettin' hungry anyway." Jimmy began rubbing his belly as if trying to console his stomach for its loss.

"Now comes the real question," Jeffrey proclaimed with somewhat of a worried look. "Which way do we go to get back to the campsite?"

"Hang on a minute," Jimmy replied while checking his front and back pants pockets. "Whew, thought I had left it at home today," he said with great relief.

"Left what?" Jeffrey confusedly exclaimed.

"My calculator, man. What else would I be looking for if I was lost?" Jimmy pretended to pull out a small, hand-sized calculator on which he began vigorously punching buttons. "You see, Jeffrey, my boy, judging by the twenty-three-degree angle at which the earth is tilted, along with the fact that we're rotating at about one thousand miles per hour…" Jimmy paused for a second, then resumed his ridiculous tirade, mumbling various complex words such as *hypotenuse* and *radii*.

"Come on, man," Jeffrey interrupted. "Quit messin' around."

"Okay, I've got it," Jimmy exclaimed with a *eureka*-like expression. "Except for the fact that I can't remember if the campsite is west or east, I think it's this way," he pronounced with one hand directed to the right and the other seriously questioning the vague assumption.

"So, just over that hill?" Jeffrey asked with an ever-growing look of concern.

"As far as I can tell."

"Man, I hope you're right. If we get lost out here, and it starts snowing again like…"

"Don't sweat it," Jimmy said calmly. "This is the right way." He tugged on Jeffrey's sleeve and pointed toward the hill they were facing. "See, doesn't it look familiar, the way the trees form a line around that lower side?"

"Yeah, I guess it does look a little familiar. That must be where we left Mark before we started wandering around these woods like gypsies."

"Exactly!" Jimmy proclaimed. "Now, let's make like gypsies again and wander our way on over to that grill."

With visions of hamburgers, hot dogs, and soft drinks dancing in their heads, the two boys frantically topped the hill. Their salivary glands seemed to be leading them to paradise as they kicked up snow with rapid procession, but the first slope merely led to another, and then another beyond it.

An unspeakable nervousness began to grow within their

chests as each new hill presented a scene that mimicked the last. The forest had turned into one vast desert of similarity, and like a mirage in the distance, it mocked their futile search for comfort and security.

"I guess we can officially say it now," Jeffrey proclaimed with a worry-ridden look of disgust. "We're lost." His limbs fell limp to his sides as he slowly descended to the ground like a worn-out prize fighter. "Come and sit by me," he tiredly mumbled.

"Man, I'm sorry I got us lost," Jimmy pronounced with a sigh after plopping down next to him.

"Don't be," Jeffrey returned. "I'm the one who wanted to look for the creek in the first place." Jeffrey picked up a handful of snow and gently squeezed it, taking notice of the way it compressed into one uniform shape. "Did you ever find any time to listen to some of that blues music I was telling you about a few weeks ago?

"Yeah, actually, I did. I ordered a CD off the internet. It was a compilation disc with Muddy Waters, Howlin' Wolf, B.B. King, and a few others that I can't remember."

"What'd ya think?" Jeffrey asked as he mashed the snow into a fine powder and let it fall to the ground.

"I liked it...well, I don't know," Jimmy returned. "It was kinda weird, definitely unlike anything I've ever heard before, with the twangy guitar play, the wailing voices, and the slow piano. It also had sort of a cloudy sound, like it came from an old radio with bad reception or something."

"The only thing that was really cool about it was," Jimmy continued, "while I was listening to one of B.B. King's songs, I could picture this young man standing under a streetlight in some big city. The rain was falling heavy and dripping off his hat onto his shiny black shoes, but he didn't seem to care. He just stood there with this blank expression on his face. He looked...poetic, I guess."

"I'm glad you liked it," Jeffrey said with a grin. "The next time you come over, we'll have to listen to some Etta James and Matt 'Guitar' Murphy. They're pretty good too."

"Yeah, I can see that happening," Jimmy murmured sarcastically. "Your parents will probably think we're a couple of sad, old men waiting for the woes of the world to take us under."

"Maybe we will be someday," Jeffrey sorrowfully pronounced as he stared at the pine trees swaying in the distance. They were wavering back and forth like tiny sailboats on an angry sea. In his younger days, Jeffrey might have focused on the triumph, but now he saw only the struggle. For the life of him, he couldn't comprehend how the forest endured the constant assault, yet always came back for more.

Perhaps the trees' will to survive was just that resilient or maybe their roots were such that no ordinary force could overwhelm them. Either way, Jeffrey knew that he couldn't relate. He sighed deeply and dropped his head in shame as the sad realization quietly took form. His life had barely begun, and he was already pleading for the struggle to end.

# 5

When Jeffrey raised his head, he noticed that the wind had ceased. All was silent now, and the earth was calm. The mountains in the distance looked down condescendingly upon the valleys and gulfs while their snow-crowned heads gleamed in the afternoon sunlight. Beneath the scattered clouds that hung motionless in the air, a faint purplish hue drifted across the skyline and came to rest upon the northern horizon.

Suddenly, the mountainside seemed more like a warm, green field than a cold, icy landscape. But the moment ended as soon as it began. The tranquility of the diffracted sunshine abruptly drifted away like the remains of a funeral pyre as the howling wind and frigid snow returned in a haunting fashion.

"Aw, man!" Jimmy protested as he jumped to his feet and slammed his toboggan to the ground. "You gotta be kiddin' me!"

Jeffrey, still lost amidst the scenery and the depressing mood that lingered nearby, was unaware that Jimmy had said anything at all.

"Hey, it might be a good idea if we start walking again," Jimmy apprehensively proclaimed while rescuing his toboggan from a frosty death. "You listenin' to me, man?"

"Yeah, I hear you," Jeffrey said as he gradually rose to his feet. Had it not been for Jimmy, he might have stayed in that same spot, resting his bones until they became just another insignificant part of the Tennessee scenery.

Then again, freezing to death was certainly not on Jeffrey's list of acceptable fatalities: overdosing on pills, now, that seemed like a very peaceful means to an end, yet it lacked the much-needed theatricality; bleeding to death could provide the melodramatic effect that an overdose lacked, but the feel of the razor blade was much too cold and impersonal; death by hanging seemed too medieval and electrocution too technological.

However, these were all minor and, therefore, acceptable flaws in the face of a greater good. Jeffrey was willing to surrender himself to all those means combined before being exposed to the prolonged pain and humiliation of freezing to death. Just the thought of shivering for hours on end as his blood coagulated into a thick, maroon jelly made Jeffrey's nerves grimace and his stomach turn.

"So, you got any ideas?" Jimmy suddenly asked.

"No, not really." Jeffrey stood motionless for a moment with an incredibly dumb expression on his face, then abruptly proclaimed, "Aw, man. I can't believe I didn't think of this before. Surely someone lives beside the creek, so all we have to do is find it and then follow the stream until we see a house."

"Ahhh, there we go," Jimmy roared. "Now we're talkin'. There's probably some bizarre poet who lives out here where he can gain inspiration from the gently soothing stream, the quiet woods, and all that other hippie stuff."

"Exactly! But we still have to decide which way the creek might be," Jeffrey pronounced while peering through the hazy snowstorm. "My judgment's been terrible so far, so you make the call."

"All right," Jimmy said as he tried to recall the position of the sun. "Rivers and stuff usually run from north to south, right? So, we definitely need to travel either east or west. I remember the sun being in that direction," Jimmy asserted while pointing toward the distant peaks, which had been visible just minutes before. "We can either go toward the sun or away from it. I'm gonna' say...toward the sun. Whatcha' think?"

"That sounds good to me," Jeffrey declared as he searched Jimmy's countenance for a sign that all would turn out well. He found no such sign. Jimmy's facial expression exuded all the uneasiness that Jeffrey felt within his own butterfly-sickened stomach. "We're not gonna find our way out of here, are we?"

"I don't know," Jimmy hollowly pronounced. "But we're dang sure gonna try. Come on. We've sat here and worried long enough."

Sluggishly the two boys set out in hopes of finding some sort of happy ending for their dismal predicament. Since they couldn't think of anything productive to say, they chose to contemplate their situations in silence. Jimmy's thoughts turned immediately to Molly. He could picture her standing at the cabin door with tears in her eyes and a sad, perplexed look on her face. He remembered she had worn her favorite red, fuzzy sweater, one he had bought for her two weeks ago on their one-year anniversary.

*She was probably expecting a wonderful day when she slid into that sweater this morning*, he thought. This caused Jimmy's spirits to reach an all-time low. Along with feeling sorry for himself, he now felt guilty for hurting the person he loved the most. He knew he had ruined her day, and that it would possibly cast a gloom over years of her life if he couldn't make it out of that blizzard.

But this was no way to think. Jimmy was not the type to dwell upon such disheartening things. Once he realized the futility of it all, he started to consider ways that he could make it up to her. *Maybe I can take her out for a nice dinner tonight and possibly throw in a movie*, he thought. *Or maybe I could...*

At the same time, Jeffrey was entertaining a very different notion. One by one, wreaths of flowers drifted through his wandering mind. Some were made of yellow and white roses interlined with pink daisies. Others had orange geraniums randomly scattered among red and white snapdragons.

Still others had red and purple roses interlined with cream-colored lilies. Each wreath was beautiful in and of itself, but when erected together they complemented one another in such a way as to form a psychedelic display of blooming colors. However, Jeffrey was not interested in the flowers. He was more focused on the bulky, awkward tombstone rising out of the ground, which read:

*Jeffrey Killingsworth*
*Beloved Son and Brother*
*1984–1997*
*May He Find Brighter Shores*
*On the Other Side*

Jeffrey took a deep breath and smiled complacently as he examined the sacred earth. Then, he began to hear people crying in the background. He looked up to see his mother and father along with William standing in the sunlight on a humid June afternoon. He wanted to scream at them, "Go home. Your lives are too important to waste them crying over someone so worthless," but the words became trapped, only to echo endlessly off the lifeless walls of the casket in which he was enclosed.

Oblivious to one another's terrifying thoughts and the freezing wind that slapped them across the cheeks, the two boys pushed on for nearly an hour. Their legs had been numb for quite some time, unlike their hearts, which beat stronger with each step. They were operating solely on a passionate will to survive, but the possibility of freezing to death still lingered in their minds. They both knew that before long, their wills would be broken, the same as their bodies.

Then, out of nowhere, a house rose on a distant hill like God's glorious throne. Jimmy and Jeffrey could barely believe their eyes. They both blinked, then blinked again, yet the house was still there. As they began to examine the wonderful sight, the anxiety and despair rolled off them so quickly that they nearly jumped out of their boots.

"Whewwwwww!" Jimmy roared like a drunken maniac in the stands at a college rivalry game.

Jeffrey joined in with a "Waahoo" and a "Yeaaaah" before breaking into a medley of dances such as the robot, the worm, and the Harlem shake. Jimmy celebrated his great fortune by pumping his fists wildly in the air and shuffling his feet in the snow while he hummed the theme music to *Rocky IV*. When the excitement wore off to some degree and the words "we made it!" finished echoing off the distant peaks, Jeffrey and Jimmy raced toward the house on the hill.

The godsend was positioned right along the creek, exactly like the two boys had imagined. Other than being run-down a little, the house was a specter of elegance, or at least the empty woods made it appear so. It was composed of a light-colored oak with huge logs running from the base to the roof. The first story assumed the appearance of an all-encompassing porch with a set of wicker chairs and a checkerboard table while the windowed-out second story loomed over the surrounding woods like an amateur observatory.

Instead of common asphalt shingles or expensive clay tiles, a tacky, red aluminum sheet extended itself over the monstrous figure of a home, causing it to stand out like a giant toolshed, isolated by miles and miles of the natural world and its lack of mechanical contrivances.

Jeffrey and Jimmy had stopped short to briefly admire the impressive wooden structure and to formulate a plan for coaxing the owner into a ride back to the campsite when suddenly, a man at the far end of the porch yelled, "What in the world is goin' on out here!" True to the image of the hillbilly stereotype, the old man stood with shotgun in hand, ready to blast any supposed intruder. "You boys almost got y'all selves shot," he abruptly said before stroking his long, white beard and adjusting his overalls. "Y'all ain't salesmen, are ya?"

"No sir," Jeffrey immediately replied while snickering a little at the absurdity of the question. "We're lost and about to freeze our legs off."

"Well, as long as you's two ain't salesmen, I suppose you can come inside."

Jimmy was a little reluctant to follow directly behind any man with a shotgun, so he let Jeffrey lead the way. As they entered the house, all that could be heard was the *clickety-clack* of the old-timer's cowboy boots upon the dingy and dusty wooden floor. Everywhere the *clickety-clack* led, animal heads on the wall were sure to open upon the bizarre yet homely scene.

Some were of exotic animals, such as African antelope and Asian bison, while others, such as grizzly bears and red foxes, carried more of the local color of the region. The furniture throughout the house could have been predated to a time before the last Great War, and fittingly, a television, or anything displaying technological innovation for that matter, was nowhere to be found.

It seemed the old man desired nothing more than to live in simplicity like his forefathers had done. However, the kitchen painted an altogether different illustration. It was decked out with the nicest and most expensive coffeemaker, refrigerator, oven, stove, and microwave that could be found anywhere, so much so that Jeffrey and Jimmy wondered for a moment if they had entered an entirely different home in the course of their short walk from the dining room to the kitchen.

"You boys want any coffee?" the elderly man suddenly said before correcting himself. "I mean, I think I may have some hot cocoa somewhere around here."

"Coffee sounds all right," Jimmy immediately responded. "Heck, anything warm will work right now."

"Coffee it is, then," the old man exclaimed while retrieving two mason jars from the cupboard. His hands shook terribly, and he nearly dropped one of the jars, but finally, with the help of a fiercely concentrated stare, he managed to fill each container with the hot Colombian cocoa. "Here you go," he said while shakily handing the jars to Jeffrey and Jimmy. "My name is Claude Bundy, by the way, but you can call me Ted. Great men deserve to have their names carried on."

Silence filled the room as a wave of awkwardness and fear swept over Jimmy and Jeffrey. In a moment of indecision over rushing the man or the shotgun beside him, the two boys froze like mob bosses witnessing their own execution. Suddenly, Claude exclaimed, "I'm just yankin' your chain, boys! You can call me Claude."

He chuckled, then continued. "Boy, you should have seen the look on your faces when I said that. Imagine that, me, a serial killer livin' way out here in the woods! Woohoo, that was a knee slapper! Don't worry about anything, boys. I'm as down-to-earth as any raccoon-shootin', overalls-wearin', loudmouth son of a gun around here!"

Jimmy and Jeffrey looked at each other with widened eyes, unsure whether to laugh or breathe a sigh of relief. "Man, that junk ain't funny!" Jimmy abruptly exclaimed while giving Claude a look of indignation.

"I'm sorry, boys," Claude responded. "You get as old as I am and stay out here by yourself in these woods long enough, your sense of humor gets a little off. Anyway, what can I help you boys with? Ya lost, ain't ya?"

"Yeah," Jimmy returned with a calmer tone. "We came up here on a church trip to some campsite…I think it's called Fall Creek. Anyway, we got lost in the woods and here we are."

"Hmmm," Claude responded while nodding his head and tugging on his gangly beard. "I think I know exactly where your campsite is. Heck, you're only about a mile away from it now." Claude continued to nod for a moment as if the wheels in his brain were hesitant to move after a lifetime of revelry and drunkenness. "I tell you what. I'll drive you up there. Just give me a second to fix me some firewater and find my keys. Then we'll be off."

With Claude in the lead, Jeffrey and Jimmy stepped out of the warm log house into an atmosphere that seemed strangely unfamiliar. The forces of nature that had previously represented doom and despair now presented themselves as natural and gentle processes of beauty and wonder. The wind whistled gently past the mammoth trees, wheezing at times like a sleeping child while the snowflakes fluttered through the air as if dancing in unison to a speedy waltz. Jimmy slowed his pace a little to admire the scene and whisper a brief "thank you" into the air.

He never noticed that Jeffrey had circled back around and was searching for the largest conglomeration of snow that he could find. Suddenly, in the style of an NFL place kicker, Jeffrey made precise contact with a mound of ice, projecting it all over the back of Jimmy's pants and coat. It was the most sure-fire sign that everything was okay now that the two boys were finally home-free.

"Man, that is cold as ice," Jimmy exclaimed while laughing at the irony of his joke. "You know what's colder, though?"

"What?" Jeffrey responded as he braced himself for whatever revenge Jimmy might enact upon him.

"Shotgun!" Jimmy yelled into the air. "I mean, outside window seat! Ha-ha, how do you like that?"

Jeffrey lowered his head in quiet submission, knowing that Jimmy had gotten the better of him this time around. After all, the act of calling a seat made more sense than any judgment in a court of law. So, Jeffrey walked sheepishly toward the truck, where he scrunched into the middle right beside Claude.

Within moments, the truck doors slammed shut, and the vehicle was halfway sliding, halfway driving up the embankment toward Creekside Drive. Without a care in the world or a look either way, Claude jerked the wheel to the right and spun ice and snow across the road. The boys were on their way home.

The ride along Creekside Drive was peaceful for Jeffrey and Jimmy only in the sense that they were out of harm's way. There were no comfortable silences or momentary chances to stare out at the looming hilltops because Claude never stopped talking. His topics of conversation jumped from the most mundane and tiresome to the most bizarre and exciting, without any space in between or any chance for rebuttal. The only subject he could manage to hold for longer than thirty seconds was politics.

"Boys," he said, "I'm the type that's always willin' to help my fellow man, unlike these politicians we have nowadays. Nope, they ain't no good for nobody. And they ain't out for nobody but themselves—greedy folks. Take this land out here, for instance. You think a man can come out here and get away from everything, don't ya? But ya can't, ya can't get away from them!

"Heck," Claude continued. "My great-granddaddy built that old cabin with his own sweat and blood, and it's been in my family for over a hundred years. Now I gotta pay taxes on it! And if I can't afford it, they say they're gonna take it away from me. Can you believe that? Heck, they'll probably tear it down and build an amusement park or a shopping center or some stupid crap like that! Anything that can bring in money, that's their policy, and the only one they go by. My point is… no man can find a place just for himself anymore. There's always got to be intrusion of one form or another."

Out of the blue, Jimmy nudged Jeffrey in the ribs and whispered, "See, just like I told you…the government. It's always about the government."

"What you say, boy?" Claude suddenly exclaimed.

"Aw, nothin'," returned Jimmy. "I was just tellin' Jeffrey that that's the place where we took our wrong turn."

"Oh, okay," Claude replied. "But like I was sayin', no man can find a place just for himself anymore. You…are…property! You belong to a system that will tear your heart out and feed it to the wolves. There's no care or consideration anymore. It's all about money and not about people. And if you don't buy in…well, you'll see when your time comes."

And with that Claude was silent. It was all a man could say. Of course, Jeffrey and Jimmy didn't take any of it to heart. They were young. The world lay before them like a bed of oysters, all filled with pearls, but the pearls were far from their minds. They could think of only one thing—the Fall Creek campsite—which, to their surprise, was coming slowly into view.

"Yippee!" Jimmy yelled like a five-year-old on a merry-go-round.

"I can't believe we made it back!" Jeffrey joined in. "I really can't believe it. Thanks, Claude, you can't imagine what a help you've been."

"Just helpin' out my fellow man," Claude replied.

"No, you've done more than that," Jimmy said. "I'd give you some money if I had any on me. You're a real lifesaver, I hope you know that. By the way, good luck with all that tax stuff. If they'll treat a nice guy like you the way they have…well, I have only one thing to say to that. Curse the government and all those criminals working for it."

"You know, you just might make it, boy, with that watch-out-for-yourself, skeptical attitude," Claude replied as the truck crept to a stop right behind the church van. "Y'all take care now," he said with a smile. The boys slowly got out and viewed their surroundings as if everything were renewed, refreshed, like the landscape on the first day of spring when the cold has ceased, and the sunshine has returned with the vigor needed to once more rejuvenate the earth.

Suddenly a loud, grinding sound and a tremendous boom filled the air as Claude's truck rumbled off down the hill.

Jimmy laughed and exclaimed, "Good old Claude! He sure was depressing but funny as crap all the same!"

Jeffrey never responded. He was staring down the hill at Natalie and Johnny, still huddled together like before, still clinging to one another as if they were witnessing some apocalyptical moment. For a second, Jeffrey wished he was still stuck in the woods. *I would probably be dead by now*, he thought and dropped his gaze slowly toward his feet.

"Thank the Lord!" Brother Rodney exclaimed. His outburst from the bottom of the hill reached the heavens much faster but with unequal power as the brief, sincere, silent prayer that followed. Without another word, he broke out into a full sprint like a child chasing an ice-cream truck. He was wearing a look of extreme joy and total relief. His relief stemmed from the fact that his job security was intact, once again.

His joy, which originated from a greater and nobler source, was due to the notion that his flock was once again safe and sound, as it should be. Like in his glory days of old, he traversed the snowy, mountainous terrain with tremendous agility and speed, dodging sharp stones and small divots, and within an instant was keeled over, gasping for air in front of Jeffrey and Jimmy.

"Boy…am I…glad…to see…you guys," Brother Rodney uttered between successive wheezes. "Just…give me…a second here…so I can give y'all…a big hug." Brother Rodney, along with Jimmy and Jeffrey's help, stood upright, breathed in deeply a few times, then proceeded to hug them like they were two prodigal sons. "Thank God almighty!" Brother Rodney cried tearfully. "These sons of mine were dead and are alive again! They were lost, and now they are found!"

Brother Rodney, feeling a little embarrassed for his uncharacteristic outburst and untimely quotation of Scripture, reluctantly released his grasp slowly and wiped the tears from his cheeks. "Well, I'm sure y'all are hungry," Brother Rodney suddenly voiced. "I wrapped up your plates in tinfoil so they'd stay warm, but they may need to be warmed up a little. Come on, I'm sure the others are dying to see you."

The three of them stumbled toward the campsite in unison, each one struggling in his own way to find the steps (amongst the hidden holes and blunt rocks) needed to complete the trip. Once they reached the bottom of the hill and looked up, they found Molly standing there, frozen in time with tears streaming down her chubby cheeks.

"I thought… I was afraid I'd never see you again," she mumbled, almost incoherently. Jimmy walked over to her slowly, captivated by the butterflies in his stomach and the adoring look on her face. Without a word, he closed his eyes and kissed her gently on the lips.

"Perhaps Molly and Jimmy feel a little more strongly about each other than they originally thought, or at least originally put on," Brother Rodney said with a smirk. "Come on, let's leave them to it."

Brother Rodney's words fell on shellshocked ears, yet Jeffrey followed closely by his side, nevertheless. His obsession over the heartbreaking situation with Natalie, rather than his own two feet, seemed to carry him forward to the quaint, beautifully positioned campground, where he dreaded that his own personal tragedy was about to be acted out.

They were only a few yards away, and already Jeffrey sensed that Natalie couldn't care less. He stared into her eyes, longing to be adored, loved, if nothing else pitied, but her empty gaze possessed nothing more than a well-controlled, phony indifference. Rather than running to him or screaming out ecstatically or…anything, she merely shook off Johnny's hold and walked back toward the cabin without a word.

*Perhaps thousands of people throughout history have had their hearts broken right here in this very place*, Jeffrey thought as the life ran out of him. He felt the pain of the moment intensely, yet he never fully realized that an essential part of him died on the very spot in which he stood, leaving behind a void that could only grow larger and more wrathful with time.

Like a sound monotonously reverberating through a cavern, Jeffrey gradually departed from his sorrowful reverie and somewhat reclaimed consciousness of his surroundings, and for good reason. An uproar of immense proportion was gathering at his very heels. Jimmy, followed by Molly, had just reached the sacred campground, where all evidence of any misfortune or tragedy disappeared.

Laughter and praise filled the air along with Mark's obnoxious claims that Jeffrey and Jimmy had the worst sense of direction in the history of the world. Madison even appeared in all her splendor to catch a glimpse of the seemingly impossible.

Pretty soon, a huddle had been formed around Jimmy so that everyone could hear the great tale of their long, heroic walk home. Jeffrey could only make out "oohs" and "aahs" and see various hands being raised from his slim vantage point on the outskirts of the crowd.

Every once in a while, Jimmy would look back in search of his fellow pioneer, but after failing to see him anywhere within or outside of the rambunctious circle, he would turn back and resume his telling and retelling of certain parts of the story. "It was insane, man!" he would yell every once in a while to raise the tension.

While standing on the outer reaches, half-listening to all the commotion, Jeffrey thought of entering the cabin a million times, but he could never get up the nerve to face the possibility that Natalie truly didn't care. Standing there motionless, he felt as if he was alone in some vast ocean with only the empty sea to hear his cries and the endless waves to mock his pain. With the exception of Jimmy, Brother Rodney, and possibly Natalie, he knew (more than felt) that no one really cared for his return.

As Jeffrey was contemplating his unimportance, Brother Rodney gently tapped him on the shoulder and said, "How about a hamburger? I know you must be hungry." Realizing the significance of the gesture, Jeffrey complied and followed Brother Rodney into the cabin. To Jeffrey's surprise, Natalie was standing in the kitchen, red-eyed and rosy-cheeked, warming up the plates for him and Jimmy.

"I'm glad you're all right, Jeffrey," Natalie muttered between sobs as she turned to face him. "Thank God you're all right!" She embraced him tightly and buried her head in his chest for a few seconds while trying to regain control of her emotions.

"Don't ever scare me like that again!" she exclaimed. After releasing her grasp and blinking rapidly several times to clear the tears from her eyes, she smiled contentedly at Jeffrey. "Oh, I almost forgot. Here's your hamburger," she suddenly whispered in a cute fashion while crinkling her face up like a little girl.

Before Jeffrey could even say thank you or grab the paper plate, he and his hamburger were thrown to the ground by the swinging wooden door of the cabin. Jeffrey surmised that good old Claude was the subject of conversation at that point because the mob was laughing hilariously as they nearly trampled him underfoot. The harder they laughed, the angrier he became.

Once again, he felt pushed to the side and out of rhythm with everything and everyone around him. He was on his feet within an instant, ducking and dodging like a heavyweight champion in Madison Square Garden, but he could never seem to stretch his neck around the horde gathered before him. He even stood on his tiptoes, but Natalie was nowhere to be found. He merely wanted to express how thankful he was for her words, but that was an absurdity that couldn't exist within Jeffrey's ill-fated, estranged world.

Luckily, though, he did find his hamburger lying on the ground underneath one of the stuffed bear heads. Jeffrey picked it up and blew it off a little, wondering how jealous the bear would be if he were still alive. He knew that according to the "five-second rule" with dropped food, he didn't quite make the cut, but he was so hungry that it didn't even matter.

Before even taking a bite, Jeffrey glanced over the chaotic scene with disgust, then slipped out the door. He found it to be peaceful outside. "Forget 'em," he muttered while taking a huge bite out of his burger. "It's nicer out here anyway."

## ❦ 6 ❦

The nighttime sky bloomed before Jeffrey like a luminous halo sparkling with blinding magnificence. An endless array of stars illuminated the sky from infinity to infinity. Jeffrey had never seen so many in his life. It reminded him of a song his mother used to sing to him when he was younger. As he began to hum the tune, a cold wind whispered past him and through him. *I hope my parents are having fun at the party,* he thought.

*I bet my dad's telling some wacky joke right now,* Jeffrey continued, *and my mom is standing by his side with beautiful, glistening eyes patiently waiting for the punch line to arrive so that she can bless the room with her kind, gentle laugh.* Jeffrey began to speak aloud. "I wonder if William is having some wild party, and he's getting nervous about Mom and Dad maybe coming home." Jeffrey laughed and genuinely smiled for the first time in a long while. "But I bet none of them are seeing what I'm seeing right now."

The euphoric glimpse that Jeffrey had caught or seen—the stars, the calm, rippling wind, the kind thoughts of his parents and brother—was something he desperately tried to hold on to. He hoped it would absorb and intoxicate him and preserve a seat in his memory forever. But it was gone in an instant as the cabin door opened rapidly.

"Time to go, everyone!" Brother Rodney proclaimed. "I've got most of the stuff packed up already, so just make sure you don't leave anything that you brought along with you! Natalie, can you make sure the oven is turned off, please? Oh, and most importantly, Jimmy, Jeffrey, make sure you don't get lost on the way to the van." Brother Rodney snickered to himself and breathed another sigh of relief.

The youth group, following closely and attentively behind Brother Rodney, climbed the hill toward the van very carefully. Jimmy was holding Molly's arm to make sure she didn't fall, Johnny was nearly smothering Natalie to death so that neither wind nor snow nor natural disaster could touch her, and Mark was continually reaching for Madison's hand or sleeve with no success.

All of them were being very careful not to step in one of the holes or trip over one of the rocks, all of them except for Jeffrey who was still staring wide-eyed at the sky, not worrying a bit about any of the bumps in the road ahead.

Still admiring the heavens, Jeffrey stumbled a little, like a drunk alone in a dark, lonesome alley. When he finally came to, he realized his daydreaming had placed him up front with Brother Rodney in the van. Everyone else was coupled up from front to back on leather, benchlike seats, taking up more than enough room to accommodate Jeffrey. Jeffrey noticed this, but he didn't say a word. He breathed deeply, swallowed his anger, then boarded the van feeling like a stranger linked to the other passengers in the oddest of ways.

During the ride home, Brother Rodney tried to talk to Jeffrey, first about normal, day-to-day things, then about sports and popular movies, and finally about the serious stuff like God, religion, and life itself. Jeffrey did his best to keep up while providing empty, preselected stock answers, but his head was somewhere else, a deserted island where he hoped to be stranded forever.

He was still hunting with wild eyes for that euphoria that had passed him up. Suddenly, sounds from the back of the van distracted him. At first it sounded like someone was smacking on some candy or gum, but then the hushed moans arrived.

*Surely they're not making out in the back of the church van,* Jeffrey thought to himself. He laughed a little, thinking that Jimmy had lost his mind. He tried looking in the side mirror for a view to the back, but this was no good. So he turned all the way around in his seat and lifted himself up a little, but the sight nearly choked him.

Jimmy and Molly were asleep in the back. Natalie and Johnny were the ones engrossed in each other. Jeffrey turned back around quickly and grasped hold of the seat belt, hoping it could secure more than just his physical being. He rocked back and forth, still holding on for dear life while trying to chase the image out of his brain.

"Is something wrong, Jeffrey?" Brother Rodney asked apprehensively as he swerved a little in the road.

"No, I'm just ready to get home. I just wanna go home. I just wanna go home." Jeffrey didn't notice that he had begun to repeat himself. It was almost like a chant, one he was ritualistically whispering to himself to make the time fly and the image stray. He looked up at the somewhat foggy windshield as he was chanting and noticed he couldn't breathe. While he choked and wheezed on his own sickness and depredation, he narrowed his eyes in an attempt to focus on something far ahead.

The road was so straight and solid that it seemed to have no end. It appeared to be repeating itself, like it would go on forever, taking him and his panic with it. Suddenly, the lights along the highway began to look strange, first a little hazy, then blurrier and blurrier until they all bled together into one strange and horrifying fluorescent red blaze.

He closed his eyes again and tried to breathe slowly, in… and…out, whew, in…and…out, whew. Brother Rodney's voice was distant, slurred, barely audible. Everything felt disastrous and guilt-ridden—the good things, the bad things, everything. Terrifying thoughts sped along the monstrous electrical wires in his brain: *Life is torture. There exists always, without stop or momentum, and without bounds, the uneasiness of life and all it brings with it.*

*We are all born to tread water*, Jeffrey continued thinking, *our heads barely above the surface, until we ultimately succumb to the fatigue and drown within the pool of our own misfortune. I must be going mad. Now I will be alone forever.* Jeffrey could not grasp, let alone control, what was happening inside of him. *Is this even me?* he wondered, as if some strange form of transcendence had taken him to an alternate universe or hell. It all seemed so absurd and twisted. He didn't think this way, and yet, he did.

He opened his eyes again, but everything was still in a panic, bleeding together, monstrously repeating itself. He had hoped he was wrong—that the road would still be materializing in the distance, that the lights would still be burning along the highway, that the yellow markers would still be glowing and guiding fellow travelers—but he wasn't wrong. Everything had changed.

His hallucinations raged like uncaged animals, like fallen angels, like fiery dragons. *I think I may be losing it,* Jeffrey pondered. He violently forced his eyes to close, fearing that the road would continue to go on forever, the monstrous thoughts forever going on. He silently pleaded for a death that would wipe away all remembrances, all worries, all of life.

While Jeffrey sat trapped in a flood of anxious and awful thoughts, Brother Rodney was simultaneously watching the road, adjusting his rearview mirror, and hollering at Natalie and Johnny in the back. He put a stop to their seemingly immoral, destructive, and inconsiderate behavior instantly as the van rolled on down the highway. Consequently, the remainder of the trip was filled with an eerie, awkward silence.

Jimmy and Molly were sound asleep in the back, Natalie and Johnny were sitting slightly apart, frozen in shame and embarrassment like stones, Mark was still looking for the right words to say to Madison, and Brother Rodney sat silently in prayer for all the youth but mostly for Jeffrey.

Once they reached Sunnyside Baptist Church, Jeffrey opened his eyes upon a world that felt vaguely familiar. Suddenly, he noticed he could breathe again. The panic had left him, but only temporarily it seemed, as if it owned an eternally reserved box seat within his mind and could come back to visit any time. Nevertheless, the demonic force was gone, and Jeffrey felt as if he had shed his skin.

Knowing he was home again, safe from the outside turbulence, a warm, bubbly feeling flowed over Jeffrey's being. *Maybe things will look up after all*, he thought as he hopped out of the van. He was wrong.

His brother, William, was standing there, stupefied, with a look of impending doom. Disaster continuously ran across his face like an electrified billboard. Jeffrey stopped in full force, unwilling to face what he already surmised to be true. William approached him silently with sluggish, unsteady steps, then told him that their parents were dead. Neither of them broke down crying immediately. The shock and disbelief lasted long enough for Brother Rodney and the other kids to pass by, casting odd glances their way.

Then Jeffrey leaned into his brother's chest and began to sob uncontrollably. William hugged him tightly and swayed back and forth as his tears fell into Jeffrey's already damp hair. There was nothing either of them could say or do to ease the pain or forego the next month or year or lifetime of grievous lucidity.

$$7$$

It was unseasonably warm for a December afternoon in Dahlonega, Georgia, when Mr. and Mrs. Killingsworth were laid out in adjoining caskets on the sunlit green lawn of Bakersfield Cemetery. The church service had gone as well as could be expected. Brother Thomas had spoken of the car accident in terms of a sadly predestined event rather than an unexplained, hopeless tragedy, while tying it in to a seemingly appropriate passage of Scripture for the occasion.

"Psalm sixteen, verses nine and ten," he declared in a charismatic, booming voice, "says this: 'Therefore, my heart is glad and my tongue rejoices; my body also will rest secure, because you will not abandon me to the grave, nor will you let your Holy One see decay.'"[2] His purpose, which was carried out with eloquent language and heartfelt sympathy, was to contrast the believer's view of death with that of the nonbeliever's. It was something the Killingsworths would have desired, he claimed.

Now, as Jeffrey sat next to this brother in the special green-cushioned chairs reserved for relatives and close friends of the family, he could hear Brother Thomas's voice running through his head like a gentle stream flowing over worn and ancient rocks, "For it is not death that we seek, but when found, it is not to be feared."

With eyes closed, Jeffrey nodded to himself in agreement, but only to the second part. When he looked up, he saw the caskets being lowered into a pair of dark chasms beside two neat piles of dirt hidden by blankets of shiny, lime-colored turf. With every descending inch, Jeffrey felt the pangs over and over in unison with the mechanical cranking of the gears that would forever hide his parents beneath the cold, quiet earth.

Once the caskets reached a certain depth and the gears ceased to turn, Brother Thomas said in a slow, solemn voice, "Ashes to ashes, dust to dust," then asked the group to bow their heads for prayer. In contrast to his sermon, he was unable to find the perfect words. Perhaps he had lost them in the ride over, when the blackness of the hearse seemed to smear its ugliness onto everything it passed. Or perhaps they had fluttered down like fallen leaves into the terrifyingly empty holes in the ground.

Wherever they were, they weren't coming out of his mouth anymore, issuing hope and faith. The perfect words of ease and comfort were lost forever. As the pastor closed his prayer with a few clichés and well-known verses, he looked up at the faction in embarrassment. "Everyone should convene at the Killingsworth house for the funeral reception," he squeakily pronounced.

When the crowd began to disperse, the finality of death and the vacuity it leaves behind became all too real for Jeffrey. He wanted to shout at them, *"Stay! Stay! Just a moment longer!"* as if the dead could still rise in modern times. But he knew it was no use, just as he knew that he would never see his parents again on this temporal earth. All he would have of his beloved mother and father now were wonderful, but constantly fading memories, and expensive marble headstones to decorate like false idols on a foreign shore.

As William led Jeffrey away from the gravesite, it appeared

as if he had suddenly grown from a goofy seventeen-year-old into a well-molded, mature man, all within a few days. He carried a solemn look, a look of new responsibility, a look that one must adopt once childish things are put away for good. His perfectly creased black suit seemed to fit him perfectly, covering up the formerly awkward posture and lanky limbs.

His eyes were still a light brown, but they appeared deeper somehow, blacker in some way. He held the passenger door open for Jeffrey once they reached the car, then grudgingly rounded the front end of the red Toyota Camry as if in preparation to take the most uncomfortable drive of his life.

"Things will get better, Jeffrey," William said in disbelief as he cranked up the car and let it idle gently. "But it's gonna take some time to adjust to all of this, whatever all of this is or becomes or whatever. The important thing to remember is that we gotta stick together now. We're not going to move to Aunt Louise's or Uncle Billie's or anywhere else. We're staying right here! I'm gonna take care of you, whatever I have to do. That's the way it will have to be. That's the way it's gonna be. It's just us now, buddy."

"Okay," Jeffrey replied as the car revved forward up the hill. "Okay." The remainder of the ride was silent except for William's slight humming of "The Old Rugged Cross." Jeffrey mostly sat there, looking out the window, swallowed by his destructive, looming thoughts. He wondered what it would be like when his parents' bodies began to decay. Though their spirits were long gone—he had total confidence in that fact— he wondered if their physical remains were lonely down there.

He wondered if he had said good-bye to them in a loving manner or if he had simply taken the moment for granted because he had expected to see them always. He wondered what they thought about as the car slid on the ice and flipped over the guardrail. He wondered if they were scared. He wondered why God would take them away just like that, in the blink of an eye. He wondered if God even cared.

Before Jeffrey knew it, he and William had arrived at their old, familiar house. It was impossible for either of them to look at it the same. William parked in a different place than his mother had ever parked the car, and they got out, ducking their heads like hooded hermits in the effort to avoid every possible recollection that the scenery demanded. Cars began to line up in the driveway and along the road as William and Jeffrey entered the house. Jeffrey thought how odd it was that all the cars arrived in a scattered pattern, but still almost simultaneously.

*Perhaps Aunt Louise took the long route around Fowler Avenue while Uncle Willie took the less scenic, but more direct route down Baker Street*, he thought. *Then again, there is always Autumn Avenue or Lullwater Road or even Flamingo Drive, though you would have to be an idiot to take that way to the house.* Jeffrey began to count all the different ways to get from the cemetery to his family's home until he ran out of fingers. *Perhaps they all took different routes*, he pondered, *only to arrive at the same cursed place.*

At first, Jeffrey considered that maybe this idea could be a metaphor for life. *All the cars had formerly been in unison*, he reasoned, *following a creepy, metallic shadow to a horror-filled sight, but now they were all scattered like they had a mind of their own, like all unity and order was lost.* Jeffrey could imagine the metaphor reaching into a dark pit, waiting for some meaning to grab its hand.

*Yet...yet*, his mind continued, *they all arrived at the same point at the same time*. Jeffrey stared at the grandfather clock at the end of the hallway, repeating the word *time* in his mind over and over again, envisioning the slowly ticking hands ultimately bringing understanding and consolation.

However, the clock merely sat there, mocking Jeffrey with its ancient wisdom and incessant ticking. Suddenly his face became distorted with anger and frustration as he roared out loud, "This is not fair!" His petty, childish metaphor was nothing more than a feeble attempt to find meaning in something that was meaningless. The painful truth was obvious to him. No one was ever in unison following any type of sick, stricken figure to a place of sadness—at least not on purpose—and no one ever arrived at any one point simultaneously.

*I wouldn't be surprised*, Jeffrey brooded, *if people never arrived anywhere at all…or even if everyone just sort of sat around biting their fingernails or twiddling their thumbs in confusion and desperation, even after death.*

The scattered and disarrayed talk began as soon as family members and friends exited their vehicles. The phrase "it's just such a tragedy" seemed to bounce from mouth to mouth, followed by "and with those two boys left pretty much alone." It would have been customary for William and Jeffrey to act as proper hosts and greet everyone at the door, but instead they just left the door ajar, letting everyone enter and ramble through the house as they wished, looking for the refreshments and finger food that the church had previously brought over.

Jeffrey secretly sat at the top of the stairs, virtually out of view from the crowd below him, and watched the commotion, all the while hoping that William was downstairs in some sort of position to keep the company occupied.

From his hidden vantage point, Jeffrey saw relatives whom

he hadn't seen in years. Aunt Louise, dressed nicely in an expensive black pantsuit, scampered by in her well-to-do manner. Her husband, Uncle Harry, was following so closely behind that his out-of-date, double-breasted black ensemble almost blended in with his wife's glamorous array. Uncle Willie was there alone, wandering around like a lost dog in a suit he had bought ages before.

Jeffrey remembered that Uncle Willie's wife had died a few years back. Uncle Barry and Aunt Harriett, wearing identically patterned clothes, him in the plainest of suits and her in a gloomy-looking, long black dress, stood in place talking loudly about the decline of American politics and economic strategy to a few of the Killingsworths' friends. *At least they are discussing something other than the obvious, ugly pink elephant in the room*, Jeffrey thought.

Among the other relatives and friends of the family, Jeffrey could barely recognize any of them. After all, he hadn't seen most of them in a very long time. Whenever he had met them in the past, the events had turned out to be little more than fleeting occurrences, so fleeting in the past, and now so fleeting in the present, that the scene began to look like a blurred photograph or a view seen from behind the stained-glass windows in an old Catholic church.

The voices of the guests, chaotically echoing throughout the house and up the stairwell, seemed to blend in perfectly with the surreal imagery that was gliding in and out of Jeffrey's perspective and consciousness.

---

"But life must go on!" someone suddenly blurted out in the dining room as the revelation that "time heals all wounds" was slowly realized by several guests in the kitchen. Natalie could hear all these petty, uncomforting comments as she explored the house looking for Jeffrey. She passed by William in the hallway and indicated her sympathy with a slight nod and closure of the eyelids before rounding the bottom of the stairway to see if Jeffrey was in his room.

She climbed the stairs rapidly, anxious to see him and make sure that he was all right. When she reached the top, she saw Jeffrey just sitting there in a daze, like he was trying to detach from a violently shifting world.

"I'm very sorry for your loss, Jeffrey," Natalie said before the mascara began to run from the corners of her eyes. Jeffrey looked up at her, as if awakening from a coma, and began to cry, as well. He patted the floor next to him, and she sat down like she had a million times before in the very same spot. As she put her arm around him and began rubbing his back, Jeffrey leaned into her like a child to his mother. She rubbed his head with her other hand and kept repeating, "Shhhhh, it's gonna be okay. Everything is gonna be okay."

Jeffrey could do nothing more than close his eyes and pray she was right. Her soft body and warm touch soothed him in a dreamlike fashion. She sat with him for close to a half hour, but it felt like only a moment, just a flicker in the dimness in which he sat. There was no time and no way for Jeffrey to express how he felt. He simply buried himself—his thoughts, his dreams, his feelings—under her soft caresses, trying to appreciate the flicker for all it was worth, for he knew that she would be gone soon, so much sooner than was necessary for the wounds to heal, so much sooner than the end of time.

And just like that, Natalie said good-bye, stroked Jeffrey's hair one final time, then grabbed the banister for support as she raised her perfect figure to full height. "I'll tell Jimmy where to find you, if that's okay," she said while parting.

"Okay," Jeffrey softly replied as he made eye contact with the person whom he knew so well, the only person who could make all his pain and anguish fly away. He watched her descend the staircase, listening to every *click* of her heels until there was silence, and Jeffrey knew he was alone again.

Suddenly, he heard his name being uttered by several people in the hallway. He knew the sound came from family members roaming the house, trying to find him so they could deliver the most important funeral gifts of all—unfelt consolations and unsound advice.

In a panic, he scurried to his room and locked the door. As he turned around, he saw his NFL pajamas lying on the bed. He walked over, sat down, and began fumbling with them. Pretty soon he was rubbing the pajamas softly across his face and taking in the smell of the detergent that his mom had used ever since he was a young child.

He wasn't crying or thinking about the strength of the NFL players anymore. Power or vigorousness no longer seemed important. He allowed himself to be submerged into his own weaknesses, like an old man slinking into a warm bath of relaxation and forgetfulness.

The knocking at the door followed by several voices in the hallway disrupted his plunge. "Jeffrey!" they all shouted disharmoniously. "Jeffrey!" He didn't say a word or move a muscle, as if staying silent and still would hide him from the nuisance and chaos outside. Then the doorknob began to wiggle, a little here, a little there, then violently. *Jeez, how stupid can people be?* Jeffrey thought. *Don't they realize that the doorknob is not gonna turn the thirtieth time if it doesn't turn the first?*

He grew angrier and angrier until he finally blew his top and yelled, "Leave me alone! Just leave me alone!"

His family treated it like a shock heard 'round the world. Jeffrey could hear them all inhale deeply as if they were exceedingly offended by his foul language and fiery attitude. He could have sworn one woman screamed, "Well, I never!" but then he reconsidered. *People don't really say high-class, bourgeois things like that anymore, do they?*

Pretty soon, the hallway outside of his bedroom door was silent again. The family members' safari had ended in disappointment. *Now they're trying to hunt down William amongst the dark corridors and hidden passages*, Jeffrey imagined. Suddenly there was another knock at his door, but this time it was of normal resonance and set to a hip-hop–like beat. He knew it had to be Jimmy, so he got up and answered the door. He told him to come in quickly, slipped past him in order to duck his head out into the hallway, looked both ways, then shut the door almost silently.

Jeffrey moved to the bed sluggishly and tossed the pajamas to the floor. Jimmy sat in an old rocking chair facing the bed. The rocker appeared to be designed for those peculiar old women who possess the wisdom of the ages, but Jimmy failed to encompass any of their qualities. He possessed neither wisdom nor age nor voodoo formulas nor spiritual peace. He also seemed to be lacking his normal array of jokes and blunders. Filled with the fear that he had no way of raising his best friend's spirits that day, he simply sat there in silence, waiting for the words that would not come.

"It's okay," Jeffrey muttered. "I know it's your thing to be funny and entertaining, but you don't have to be right now. We can just sit here and be quiet if you'd like."

"I do want to say I'm sorry," Jimmy replied. "I can't imagine how tough this must be, and I feel awkward as heck trying to come up with something that will make you feel better, but I'm not gonna tell you some lame stuff like those people downstairs probably tried to say. This stinks. That's about the best way I can put it."

"Yeah…it does," Jeffrey responded. "The only thing I keep thinking about is…why all of this at once? I mean, the Natalie thing, the feeling-sad-all-the-time thing, and then this, to top it all off. What in the world! I feel angry and sad and a bunch of other things I don't even understand."

"I hear you, man. I have no philosophical or religious answers to any of that stuff. Heck, even if I did, I would probably just keep my mouth shut anyway. All that philosophical mumbo-jumbo doesn't help in a time like this. I remember one time in class, Mr. Glitsky asked if I had anything to add to Plato's argument. I stood up and said that all these idiotic philosophers are like dogs chasing their own tails, though no tails exist. Is that crazy or what?"

"Not too crazy," Jeffrey said in the midst of a brief laugh. "It actually makes a lot of sense. You standing up and saying that crap is kinda crazy, though." It appeared that Jimmy had pulled off a miracle again. He once again had something up his sleeve that maybe even he didn't know about. If only for a brief moment, he did make Jeffrey feel better. *Maybe it was the rocking chair that gave him sudden wisdom and inspiration,* Jeffrey thought.

"I think with that, I'm gonna leave, Jeffrey boy. Not to say I'm trying to leave on a high note, but…I just think you need some time alone, and anyway, I don't know how to help… So, I'll see you tomorrow, right?" Jeffrey was lost in thought and left the question hanging in the air. "Right?" Jimmy repeated a little louder.

"Yeah, yeah, sure. We'll find something to do. Maybe we'll go jump off a bridge or run out in front of a train," Jeffrey slightly mumbled with the straightest face possible and cloudy eyes that attempted to deconstruct the pattern on the wall-paper.

"Ooooooookaaaaaaay, that's not quite what I had in mind, but, ummm...sure, we'll find something to do," Jimmy said with uncertainty and distress. When he closed the door behind him, he paused for an instant, caught between the decision to collapse in tears or call for help. Jimmy did neither.

On his way down the stairs, he ran into Brother Rodney and Brother Thomas. After a short pause, he said quietly, "I don't think Jeffrey wants to talk to anybody right now. He probably just needs to be alone and sort all this stuff out. He should be better tomorrow. I'll try and bring him by the church sometime this week, even if I have to drag him there." Jimmy squeezed past them along the stairwell. Looking back, he said, "By the way, that was a great sermon, Brother Thomas. I thought it fit the occasion perfectly."

Brother Thomas and Brother Rodney weren't sure whether to take Jimmy's advice or not. They stood there in suspended animation for a while, then descended the stairway in silence. They immediately headed for the front door to speak in private outside. "So, what do you think about this whole situation, Rodney?" Brother Thomas said in his monotonous voice.

"Well, I think William will be fine. He's older and more stable. Jeffrey, on the other hand, has been having problems of some sort or another for the last few months," Brother Rodney replied.

"What sort of problems?" Brother Thomas interrupted.

"Well, I guess you would call them emotional or mental or both. You know I'm no psychologist or psychiatrist, so I'm not really sure. What I am sure of is that he needs some counseling and possibly some professional help."

"Uh-huh, I see. So maybe when he comes by the church or if we have to physically come out here ourselves, we can lightly touch on some of these matters."

"Definitely. That sounds like the best route to take, Thomas. But we will have to be delicate. We don't want to jump-start any type of rebellious attitude."

"Certainly not. I think it will all work out just fine. Besides, we've probably got a few days before we have to speak to him, so I'm sure we can put our heads together and come up with the right words."

"Yeah, I think so, too," Brother Rodney concluded.

The ministers had already begun walking to their cars along with the rest of the funeral party. With the exception of Brother Rodney and Brother Thomas, the family and friends of the late Robert and Stacy Killingsworth were behaving strikingly odd, as if they had been forced to endure some undeserving, exhausting climb to the most distant hilltop or descent into the most terrible crevice. Their heads hung low, and they spoke in breathless whispers.

The women in the group wore gothic-looking, with vampire-like designs in the corners of their eyes and along the outer edges of their cheeks, while the accompanying men carried loose, sagging faces and deep, dark bags under their eyelids. As if supported by invisible canes, they crept toward their cars and their freedom like a league of monsters with ugly masks and evil, unseen motives.

Yet strangely, their feet moved swiftly. There appeared to be a poorly hidden, mysterious joy resounding throughout the group. It was a false sense of joy that could only be produced by the lowest of life forms in a slowly moving time of desperation. The joy grew larger and larger as each passing second assured them that the realization was true—the long-dreaded, awful incident was over. They could now scurry back to their normal lives and repress or forget altogether this terrible day.

Jeffrey and William, on the other hand, could not. They sat together on Jeffrey's bed, telling stories about funny things their dad had done or said, or the sweet way their mom had always made them feel safe and important. After close to an hour, William abruptly stopped and said, "I think I might go to bed, Jeffrey…or at least go lie down and try to sleep."

"Okay," Jeffrey responded. "I guess I should do the same."

"Good night. I'll see you in the morning. I'll cook us a big breakfast, and we'll talk some more about all of this. I think the more we talk about it, the better off we'll be."

"Yeah, probably," Jeffrey said without conviction. "Well, good night to you too. Sweet dreams." As William closed the door, Jeffrey realized that he didn't want to talk about it or think about it or dream about it or hear about it anymore. The last few months of his life resembled, more than anything else, a blurry hallucination, or some virtual reality experiment gone terribly wrong. Misfortune had swooped in like Death upon a pale horse, bringing with it the overwhelming feeling that all good things would end and that happiness would be no more.

Feeling calamitously depressed, Jeffrey sighed deeply, then placed his feet one at a time onto the cold, wood floor and rose from the bed like a zombie. He tiptoed down the hallway and entered his parents' room. He couldn't bear to look around, so he immediately rushed to the bathroom and set his eyes upon the medicine cabinet above the sink.

As he opened it, he looked inside, as if he were entering a brave new world or as if some sort of bright light was ascending to the sky. He scanned the pill labels ravenously, stopping only to consider the names he didn't recognize and the side effects that might come with the mystery drugs.

Suddenly his eyes pounced upon a bottle of Trazodone. He recalled a time period when his mom had begun to sleep very poorly at night. *These must be the pills she was prescribed*, Jeffrey thought as he read the label describing when and under what circumstances to take them. "Perfect." He snatched the bottle of sleeping pills along with a few others and dumped them all out onto the bathroom counter.

After grabbing a small paper cup and filling it with water, Jeffrey began swallowing three or four pills at a time, alternating rapidly—pills, water, pills, water—until the bathroom counter was nearly spotless. Then, he shut the medicine cabinet quietly and turned to leave the room. He scurried past the bed with his head down and entered the hallway. As soon as his feet transitioned from the warm, comfortable carpet to the cold, polished wood, the house seemed to groan and moan for a moment before falling chillingly silent.

Jeffrey stood motionless, waiting for the next frightening sound, but the house wouldn't speak. There were no monsters and no ghosts, no phantoms to haunt the emptiness that remained. There was nothing left but the still, sad music, tolling louder than ever like a giant church bell—*donggggggg… .donggggggg*—the rhythmic vibrations streaming through all things.

Jeffrey knew the music would never stop, that it would only

grow louder each day without toil, without principle, without pity. Its omnipresent nature and boundless strength would ruin, in the most chaotic of fashions, any and all chances for tranquility. Discouraged by this sudden emotionally crippling effect, Jeffrey mechanically resumed his whispering walk toward the end of the hall.

Once he reached his doorway, he disgustingly mumbled, "Happiness is a lie hyped up by fools." He looked on the floor for something to throw, but his room was spotless. Then he thought about punching the nearest wall, but he knew that wouldn't solve anything, either.

Jeffrey closed his eyes, breathed in deeply, then exhaled very slowly. *There's no reason to be angry anyway*, he thought and shrugged his shoulders in a cocky fashion. *This sadness won't follow me where I'm going.* He pursed his lips and calmly nodded his head several times while glaring into the mirror at a blurry figure seemingly miles beyond himself.

*The great gig in the sky...where all tears are wiped away*, Jeffrey continued thinking. The anger subsided, and Jeffrey's demoniacal glare began to fade as the reflection streaked and blurred across his vision. Thoughts of suicidal comfort began to surge through him, like the peaceful and powerful energy flow within the meditations of a Buddha preparing for the afterlife. Basking in this supernatural glow, Jeffrey floated toward the bed, where the cool sheets and soft blankets welcomed him for the last time.

His thoughts ran hungrily through his head, searching for a single memory or a myriad of experiences that would calm him. Finally he came to rest upon a concentrated image encompassing the numerous vacations he and his family had spent in Florida at his grandmother's house. He remembered having the most peaceful feelings within that house, but he struggled to establish any logical explanation for the treasured sentiments of his past.

*It wasn't the slight smell of mothballs in the closets or the constant smell of good Southern meals cooking in the kitchen,* Jeffrey determined. *And it couldn't have anything to do with auras, because auras only exist for people, not places.*

He bunched up the skin on his forehead and deliberated for a moment before ultimately deciding on the most feasible conclusion: *Maybe the house was so peaceful simply because that nice, old woman had lived there for so long, and now only kindness could dwell within…no evil spirits, no angry poltergeists. Yeah, that's gotta be it.* Jeffrey nearly forced himself to believe it, but he had to concede that maybe that wasn't it at all, that maybe it was something else, something so inconceivable, so immeasurable, so inaccessible that only God could grasp it.

As he pondered this mystery, he felt emotionally confused to the point of nausea, but he was also comforted to some degree by a peace that flowed from some strange and unknown place. A melancholy smile bloomed and withered upon his face while strange sensations coursed through his body like shivers up the spine.

He remembered his grandmother's constant but kind lecturing on the Holy Bible and how she claimed it contained the solutions to all of his problems. "If you read the Bible daily," she would say, "you'll find that life's problems aren't as big of a deal as you think. This wonderful and glorious God of ours can overcome any obstacle you face."

As Jeffrey reflected on his grandmother's wisdom, he began to feel tranquil and relaxed. It was if God was speaking to him through these memories. He opened the drawer to his nightstand and pulled out a relatively new, seldomly used Bible his mother had given him for his eleventh birthday.

He opened the Bible to a random page near the middle and began to read:

*For I know the plans I have for you, declares the* LORD, *plans to prosper you and not to harm you, plans to give you hope and a future. Then you will call on me and come and pray to me, and I will listen to you. You will seek me and find me when you seek me with all your heart* (Jeremiah 29:11–13).[3]

Jeffrey closed the Bible and lay back on the bed. He let his mind absorb the words and contemplate the message they sent. *Maybe God does have a plan for me*, he thought. A serene quietness expanded through his chest into his lungs as he breathed deeply.

He felt like a child being rocked to sleep as he turned onto his side and pulled his knees up to his chin. He realized that the words he had just read were meant for him, purposed for this very moment in time. He regretted this terrible act, this gorging of pills, this destruction of life. He wanted to live, but it was too late.

The pills had already dissolved in his stomach and begun to take effect. As his thoughts began to scatter and the images in his mind became distorted, Jeffrey sensed that sleep was clumsily stumbling through his doorway while Death, following closely behind, was emerging from the darkness in the hall.

## 8

Wise men say that time heals all wounds, but only fools believe that time has such a power as this. In reality, time merely obscures the wounds in a fragile cloud of forgetfulness. The capacity to disregard or repress the nightmares of the past is testament to the awe-inspiring ability of the human brain to adapt to the worst of conditions, to thrust aside all the repulsive things, to accept disaster with an optimistic stance, to simply survive. Rather than seeing the ultimate reality in things, the mind demands its own outlook and recklessly stamps an indefinite impression upon the world outside.

And so it was with Jeffrey Killingsworth as he walked the streets of downtown Atlanta with swift feet and nimble strides. With the past mostly behind him—his parents' deaths; the intense, wavelike rolls of depression and anxiety; the awkward struggles of adolescence—the future invited him with glowing gratitude. His unsuccessful suicide attempt had convinced Jeffrey that he neither could nor would die in the near future, that he was invincible, that God had alloted him the grandest and most significant of fates.

He was in his second year of college now and was doing quite well, making the Dean's List twice and hovering around a 3.5 GPA. After floating with ease through an accelerated academic program and graduating as the valedictorian of his class, Jeffrey had received an engineering scholarship from the prominent and revered Georgia Institute of Technology.

Even there, among some of the most intelligent minds in the nation, Jeffrey stood out as one of the most gifted students in the majority of his classes, in addition to being one of the most attractive, this according to his adoring female and envious male classmates. Nature had been kind to Jeffrey—he had grown into an extremely intelligent, handsome man with piercing, dark blue eyes, a tall, athletic stature, and slightly curly, shiny brown hair.

The parts of his DNA that had seemed to lie dormant for most of his life finally bloomed during the summer after his sophomore year of high school, transforming him into a star athlete, a superior student, and a heartthrob for all the girls in school. He had briefly dated a third of the cheerleaders, a few of the band members, and one of the girls on the math team. Jeffrey only had two qualifications for the girls he went out with—as long as they were pretty and could hold a decent conversation, he chased them until his tires went flat.

Unfortunately, Natalie was the only one whom he couldn't quite catch. Though he felt unshakeable in any other setting or situation, she could always rattle him. It was never her intention to do so, but due to Jeffrey's inability to climb the most idealistic and adorned pedestal he had ever built, it was frustratingly impossible for them to converse on any mutual level.

He thought about her again very briefly as he crossed North Avenue to eat at the Varsity, but not with sadness or anxiety as in the past, for nothing could phase him now—no colossal tragedy, no slight disappointment, no unfortunate surprise. His delusions of grandeur shone forth in the form of a radiating smile that shamed the pathetic and weak world beneath him.

As he reached the entrance, the intense smell of hot grease subdued him like a spell, exciting his taste buds and arousing his stomach. He looked around hungrily for Julie Carnegan, his girlfriend of nine months, but she was nowhere in sight. *Leave it to her to be late*, he thought. *Always late…always thinking only of herself.*

Her lack of punctuality and dominating egocentricity were two of the many infuriating traits that Julie possessed. In addition, she was not funny, not intelligent, not creative, and not compassionate. She reminded him of a plastic doll, terribly static, with a gaze that reflected absolutely nothing.

"People are so disappointing," Julie was known to say, "and conversations are usually a complete waste of time." Due to idiotic opinions like these, she was never altered in the least bit by any admirable advice or various trinkets of wisdom. As for heated arguments or discussions, Julie utilized the tactics of those involved in one-sided strongholds—she would stick to her opinions no matter what and change the subject or lie (both to herself and others) in order to make her points seem valid.

Her extreme shallowness caused her to walk through life as if the world either belonged to her alone or didn't exist at all. However, she was very beautiful—aside from Natalie, she was the most beautiful girl Jeffrey had ever seen. She had dazzled him from the start and dazzled him still. Julie Carnegan was living proof that beauty goes a long way and often covers a multitude of sins.

Jeffrey fumbled his thumbs and picked at his fingernails as his frustration peaked. His head rattled from side to side as if on a well-oiled swivel. A few minutes more, and he would leave. He cursed her under his breath for losing her cell phone the day before. He cursed her for being late. He cursed her for nearly everything she had ever done. Just a few minutes more, and he would be gone.

The aroma from inside seeped out continously as if from the wound of a hemophiliac, enveloping him entirely, reminding him of his hunger and, consequently, of his anger for having to wait. He thought about just grabbing some food to go and eating it as he walked down the street. Just a few minutes more, and he would leave.

Suddenly he could see her crossing the street, her long, sandy-blond hair bouncing in rhythm to the *pop* and *click* of her shoes on the street. She had on high-heeled, black open-toed shoes with strings that twisted and turned around her slender calves like vines encircling a young, blossoming tree. A black miniskirt was tightly wrapped around her thin waist and perfectly captured the curvy nature of her hips; a little lower, it contracted just enough to show her tight, tanned thighs and hamstrings.

At the top, she wore a tight, white spandex shirt that cleaved to her like a gymnast's leotard. *She is certainly something to look at*, Jeffrey thought in unison with every goo-goo-eyed man waiting for the traffic light or scurrying along the sidewalk toward an unknown future and a brand-new lustrous fantasy.

"'Ello, Jeffrey!" Julie blurted out, poorly mimicking a British accent.

Her smile was perfection, her eyes mysteriously dark, her cheeks thin and well-defined. Jeffrey was dazzled.

"I said hello," Julie pressed on.

"Oh, hey," Jeffrey responded after the enchanting moment had ended. "You look…great!" he wondrously exclaimed. His anger and frustration had departed the instant he saw her, as if a pouring, drenching rain had washed him clean.

"Well, thank you very much!" she replied cheerily with a tilt of her head and an elegant smile.

"You are more than welcome." Jeffrey grasped her arm softly and pulled her closer. They pecked one another lightly and embraced momentarily in the midst of the busy, hungry crowd. "Come on, we need to get in line," Jeffrey whispered in her ear before kissing her once more on the cheek.

The cashiers mashed keys and passed money with amazing speed while the cooks in the back flipped sizzling ground beef patties and plunged frozen variations of potatoes into fryers of rumbling grease with calculated ease. The process was organized madness, something Jeffrey loved to witness. As they slid their way into line, Jeffrey remarked, "Man, that smells good!"

"Ewwww, no way!" Julie crunched her face into a nauseated position. "I don't see why you always want to come here when all they have is this nasty, unhealthy food."

"Ah, whatever," Jeffrey replied with a quick wave of his arm downward through the air. "Greasy food is good for the soul. It's a Southern tradition, baby. So, you gonna try a burger this time, or go with the traditional French-fries-only meal?"

"French fries only." Julie's beautiful eyes were searching the menu on the board above the cooks as if a new, healthy choice might have been added overnight.

The conversation halted, and they stood in silent communion, Jeffrey unable to keep himself from caressing her shoulders, Julie happily enjoying the attention that he always gave her. The line of people evaporated quickly, and Jeffrey found himself in front of a middle-aged woman with a kind smile.

He ordered their food with speedy precision—a double cheeseburger with fries and a Pepsi for him, a small fry and a Diet Mountain Dew for her. Before the final syllables were uttered, the machine went into action. Dark green paper and small metal pieces passed from hand to hand, hamburger meat sizzled, cheese melted, fries bubbled, and in a moment, his and Julie's food lay before them on an already somewhat greasy red tray.

They spotted an empty table with ease, positioned right in the middle of the ravenous crowd. They scurried toward the seats, conscious of anyone standing around who might take their place, sat down in a musical-chairs-violent fashion, and began to eat. They didn't talk much at first, but then Julie went into a row about a girl at work gossiping to some other girl about something altogether meaningless and mind-numbing.

Jeffrey tried to steer the conversation into more serious territory—sometimes about knowledgeable subjects, sometimes about current events, most often about their relationship—but as often as not, he failed and had to listen to the monotony once again that dulled his senses and drained his desire. Ultimately, he reached a point where he was able to tune her out, giving him a chance to stare at her as if she were a strange, exotic girl whom he was seeing for the first time across a crowded room, across a lonely bar, or across a well-lit street at night.

"So, what do you think about the movies tonight?" Julie suddenly asked.

"Oh, whatever you want to do is fine with me," Jeffrey responded blindly.

"Okay, so we're on for tonight, then," Julie rebuffed while tossing her hair to the side and adjusting her top. "Great, I'm looking forward to it!"

"Yeah, me, too." He paused. "Definitely!"

It wasn't until Julie stood up to leave that Jeffrey realized their lunch date was over. He looked down to see exactly how much of his meal he had eaten and was surprised to find that most of it was gone. He had the intense feeling that time had changed, warped, in an unpleasantly relative way.

He wondered if this was due to the enjoyment of having Julie around or to the fact that his mind was mostly under-water, surfacing only momentarily to get air before plunging again into the great abyss. He knew he didn't have time to theorize or philosophize over this matter at the moment, yet his renegade thoughts kept dragging him along like a dog by the tail. Julie was saying something, and then she was leaving.

"Hey, baby," he called into the crowd that was carrying her away. "Come back real quick. There's something I need to ask you."

Julie returned with a frustrated look on her face. "What is it, baby?"

"I was wondering if you wanted to walk with me just a few blocks more."

"I just told you, baby, that I have to be back at work in ten minutes," Julie replied with confused, squinting eyes.

"Oh, crap, I'm sorry. I must have heard you wrong. This place is so dang loud sometimes." Jeffrey scanned the crowd, forcing blame upon them with his fierce gaze.

"That's okay," Julie said with a smile and a sexy wink.

"Alright," Jeffrey replied. "Call me when you get off work, then. Love you."

"Love you too, baby." Julie blew him a kiss and walked away swiftly. He studied her movements, admiring her style and dwelling upon her mystique, until she was completely out of sight. Jeffrey was dazzled.

As he sat back down to finish his meal, a strong feeling of peace and prosperity bloomed within his chest, expanding outward into the air for a moment, then collapsing back upon itself in a return to its rightful place. Their date had been a success, Jeffrey perceived, despite the intervals of dull conversation. He took a bite of his cheeseburger, chewing and reflecting, contemplating and masticating.

"The important thing," Jeffrey mumbled to himself while closing his eyes and bowing his head in a prayerlike fashion, "is that even at its worst, the conversation was comfortable and smooth, the body language was positive and inviting, and the consistent, sincere eye contact was solid and promising." These were the things of utmost importance, Jeffrey considered, especially since he planned on popping the question at some point in the indeterminate future.

He knew they hadn't been dating very long and were still relatively young. He was well aware of her faults and downfalls. Of course, they had their highs and lows like any couple, but they always seemed to come out okay, even after all the bickering, arguing, and hurtful remarks.

Jeffrey's mind centered on the fact that they were always able to rise up out of the muck, dust themselves off, and continue down the long and winding road with blinding confidence. To him, this was indisputable proof that they could make it for the long haul. From the outside, the idea of marriage seemed absurd, like a recipe for disaster, but judging from the inside, the verdict was based upon love and love alone.

Unfortunately, Jeffrey's love was no fair judge—it was rooted in rotten soil, built upon sandy ground, based on narcissism and the fear of loss. Yet it was all Jeffrey knew of romantic love, and he intended to hang on to it no matter how bad things got. Consequently, he viewed their hackneyed, cliched relationship as an extensive, grueling battle he would ultimately win.

*A walk would have been nice*, Jeffrey thought while rising from the table with the greasy red tray. He squirmed and weaved his way past fat men in work clothes; tiny, old women with shaking hands; and young girls with ketchup-covered, laughing faces,. He grinned, thinking of the silly little games he and Natalie used to play in his old house—doctor, hide-and-seek, Simon Says—and of the contests they created—mud pie bake-offs, sandpit sumo wrestling, and shadow stomping.

He remembered their pledge to grow old together and never leave each other's side, just like the pledge both of their parents had made. *Naïve promises that quickly deflate in the face of the real world*, Jeffrey thought with contempt.

Suddenly his pocket vibrated and the "Sanford and Son" tune murmured through his thin, denim pants. He knew it was Jimmy calling because of the designated ringtone. Jeffrey hurriedly dumped his leftover food in the trash, set the tray on top of the red, wooden box, and wiped his hands with a few of his leftover napkins. He plunged into his pocket with enthusiasm, snatched out his glossy, black phone, and flipped it open.

"What's up, man!" Jeffrey yelled.

"A bunch of stuff!" the voice returned with delight on the other end. "Don't you remember? The grand opening is tonight, sonnnnn!"

"Oh crap, I forgot!" Jeffrey replied. "The blues club! Dang! Me and Julie are supposed to go to the movies tonight."

"Man, forget that!" Jimmy could be heard loud and clear over the laughter and yelling in the background. "You're hangin' out with me tonight! This is my club opening, man! You gotta be there!"

Jimmy was the owner of a brand-new blues club located smack-dab in the middle of Buckhead—a very good setting for any bar. He had heard about the closing of a certain lower-class establishment named Legends several months before, and suddenly, as he sat in the tub one fine Tuesday afternoon, the idea of leasing that building occurred to him. "Eureka," he had cried out as he splashed his hands repeatedly into the bath-water, laughing triumphantly.

Though the vision had come to him in an instant, it seemed to Jimmy like it had been brewing all along, day to day, hour to hour, with every blues record he bought and every song he heard. At some indeterminate point, Jimmy had become the lonely young man under the streetlight standing in the rain with the painfully empty, poetic expression. The blues had become his music, and now the blues would become the theme of his club.

He had no problem getting the money. His parents' consistent neglect throughout childhood and well into adulthood provided the perfect opportunity for Jimmy to hit them up for some big bucks. Their guilt, lying helplessly in the form of ink on a check, transformed Jimmy's vision into a reality within a month's time.

The building was completely renovated—walls were torn down, several small bars were installed, dim inside lights were mounted, antique tables and chairs were laid out, and a huge, bright-blue neon sign reading JIMMY'S BLUES was mounted on the outside. The entire design seemed poised for the most important ingredient—the stage.

It was as if the contents of the club, from the outside sign to the individual chairs, leaned toward that piano, drum, guitar-holding, dark, mysterious place, anxiously awaited the arrival of those sad, wailing songs put to the beat of the strangest pitches and tones ever heard.

"Okay, good!" Jeffrey resumed. He could already feel his insides tickling and tingling in anticipation of the alcohol and cocaine that would naturally come with the party. He decided to skip his last class. He wouldn't be able to concentrate anyway, not now. "I'm on the way!" he proclaimed.

"Yeah, that's what I'm talkin' about!" Jimmy shouted excitedly. "Well, hurry up, then! That's right, homeboy! Skip that last class! Our topic for the day is much more interesting! We're contemplating, ruminating, speculating on a whole new thesis concerned with, ummmmm, extreme drug use!" He yelled something into the background, creating a roar of laughter, and then the call went dead.

Jeffrey knew time was his enemy. Since he had walked to the Varsity, he would have to go home in order to get his car. This would, of course, lead to an irresistibly compulsive desire to change clothes, drink a beer, and smoke a blunt before ultimately walking out the door. Catastrophically unacceptable.

He would be stuck in traffic for hours. He could picture it all now: his chest bursting open upon the freeway due to a sudden anticipatory thought or reminder of the fun ahead, his climbing frustration once the cars started honking and cutting each other off, his complete loss of sanity when the incessant slow nudging began.

"The train!" Jeffrey suddenly exclaimed. "MARTA!" If he could reach the station in time for the next subway car, everything would work out to perfection. Luckily, he had his wallet and his brain—he sometimes seemed to leave the latter at home—and he wouldn't be needing anything else. He figured he was dressed well enough.

If forced to, he could borrow some clothes from Jimmy. No big deal. As for returning home, he'd worry about that later. He could always crash at Jimmy's for the night. At the moment, the significance of future planning appeared, to Jeffrey, grossly exaggerated. Getting to Jimmy's house without a hitch was the only thing that mattered. Arriving home later and preparing for his upcoming morning classes would have to be tomorrow's lonely concern.

The race to the station seemed predestined. The crosswalk signs changed at the snap of his fingers, the large, rumbling crowd separated at the sound of his swift feet, the sidewalk became lanes on an Olympic track, the shuffle of fellow racers pushing Jeffrey forward harder and harder. He reached the station simultaneously with the subway car.

As the big, silver machine discharged its customary, loud swishing sound, Jeffrey also exhaled with a loud, wheezing gust. He struggled to catch his breath—too much smoking as of late—while he paid the cashier for a token, always conscious of the train, making sure the train was there, that the train wasn't leaving him.

"Thank you," he said to the man behind the glass.

"You're welcome. Have a blessed day," the man behind the glass returned.

"Oh, how soon until it leaves?" Jeffrey politely asked.

"Ohhh, you've got about two minutes."

"Cool. Thank you." Jeffrey scooped up the token with his right hand while digging in his pocket with his left. He pulled out a pack of Newports and a cheap Bic lighter. After retrieving one of the cigarettes, he carefully placed the neat, tight box back into his pocket. He fired up the Newport while popping the token into the slot on the revolving gate release.

As he pushed through the mechanical rotating arms, he clouded the passageway with a huge puff of smoke. Then, he immediately ducked back into the cigarette, pulling on it hard and steady, knowing he didn't have much time left before the health-conscious, surgeon general-approved, non-smoking subway car would force him to extinguish the nasty garbage.

*It seems like smoking isn't allowed anywhere these days,* Jeffrey thought as he continued to hotbox the Newport. *I wonder if they'll ban it one day and throw us to the wolves. We'll probably have to hide around corners, become shut-ins, get connections on the street, play cat-and-mouse with the police, flush out the narcs.*

Jeffrey flung the cigarette onto the ground and entered the subway car just before the doors shut. *Two minutes, my butt!* he thought as he lightheadedly plopped down into a bright blue seat catty-corner to the entrance. His excitement was contained for the moment.

He looked around at his fellow passengers with wonderment as movie scenes flickered through his head. In nearly every film he could remember, subways were depicted as the exhausted carriers of degenerate hobos, dangerous-looking gang members, sad old men and women worn out from the daily grind. To his surprise, Jeffrey saw nothing more than ordinary people—young men with baseball caps turned backward, pretty young girls with short skirts and painted lips, middle-aged executives with laptops and briefcases.

*Maybe it's me,* Jeffrey thought. *Maybe I'm the strange and weary traveler.* A look of panic and trepidation locked onto his face as he counted the metal grooves in the ceiling of the tram. *Six,* he thought. *The most awful number. A cursed car. A maiden voyage after the champagne fails to explode upon striking the ship. Why isn't there seven? Who is running this show?*

The number seven had recently become very important to Jeffrey. From numerous scriptural references, he knew it to be God's number. While walking on the sidewalks, very careful not to step on any of the cracks, he would count the various things that he passed—streetlamps, cars, trees, bushes, buildings—and section them off into units of seven. With each concluding unit, he would clear the count and release the section of seven from his weary consciousness.

He practiced this idle habit constantly—while driving, eating, even showering—and found that the number seven could always be found, counted, sectioned off, and released. Jeffrey never perceived that his tendency to count and clear numbers of objects in his head might be abnormal and a premature sign of mental illness. To him, it was nothing more than a simple, idle habit that had somehow drifted into his daily routine.

Of course, he never told anyone about this strange practice of counting sevens, just as he would remain silent toward the other passengers about the number of grooves in the ceiling of the subway car. They would never know it was a doomed car, a manufacturing mistake, and the ignorance of this would never hurt them. *It would be a shame if it did*, Jeffrey thought. *They look like such nice people.*

He especially admired the two young boys scrunched together in quiet obedience beside their young, attractive mom. He knew they had bright futures ahead of them. It was in their eyes. They would escape and live outside of the money-hungry, selfish, backbiting ideals instilled by the most powerful elites ever established on the globe. They would find happiness in love—not money—and treat their neighbors kindly. They would marry and raise unpoisoned children in a new age of technological wonder.

Like the unexplained, high-pitched noise that rang in Jeffrey's left ear from time to time, he perceived that these visions must be of some supernatural origin. They were of no prophetic value, but they were entertaining nevertheless. He set his eyes upon the old man at the end of the subway car and tried to imagine his future as well. Blank.

*Perhaps the soul of the young girl across the aisle may have something to say,* Jeffrey pondered. Blank. He tried this on several other passengers, a few times successfully, but most often not. By the end of his irrational and delusional dabbling in the future affairs of others, the train came to a halt. The ride was over.

Jeffrey rose from his seat as if lifted by the thick, subway air around him. With a brief prayer, he blessed his fellow passengers, asking that God would give them the happiness that he himself might never find, then flowed out of the separated doors. He knew that Jimmy's house was nearly a mile away, but he had plenty to think about and so many things to count that he didn't mind the walk. He could feel the alcohol and cocaine impatiently calling for him, but he knew they would wait, that they would faithfully hang on until he reached them. They always did.

### ❧ 9 ❧

Jeffrey paused for a moment in Jimmy's driveway to savor the relief, contentment, and exhilaration he felt after escaping, if only for a moment, the inner city he called home. He saw it as a wasteland of sorts where the lifeless, hard steel spread its arms arrogantly toward the sun while the soft, living lumps of flesh squashed their shoulders together and tucked their arms in tightly in order to make room for the thousands of other lumps striving to occupy the same claustrophobic space.

He looked upon the house with proud eyes in spite of the fact that the structure itself—a typical one-story, three-bedroom building composed mostly of bricks and wood—was far from impressive. However, despite its normalcy or quaintness, depending on one's point of view, it provided Jimmy with a space of his own—a space to think, feel, laugh, cry, rage, and even howl if he wished without bothering or being bothered by ten to fifteen other people surrounding him in nearly every direction.

The privacy...that was what struck Jeffrey as important, the thing that mattered most, at least for the time being. *It's strange that all houses look the same these days,* Jeffrey thought. *It's a crying shame. There's no more originality left and very little space, it seems. We should have all been born thousands of years ago. We could have been heroes of old, men of renown.*

If it weren't for the unmown lawn, unkempt bushes, and nonexistent flowers or other decorations, Jeffrey would have been forced to study the street address in order to find his current place in this world. As he approached the door, his insides began to twist and stir. He knocked lightly, then stepped back a few feet.

Scattered images from his last visit flittered within his skull. He and Jimmy had invited a ton of people over, but no one showed up, and to top it off, all three of their dope men were incognito for the night. "This is a consequence of dope dealer conferences going on," Jimmy suggested at the time.

It was a total flop, but Jeffrey and Jimmy decided to make the best of it, just the two of them. They drank and smoked their backs out until all the weed and nearly all the alcohol were gone. He distinctly recalled Jimmy throwing up at the end of the night in the bushes outside, turning back for only a moment between upchucks to say, "Save yourself."

Jeffrey looked around to see if he could remember the chosen bush while laughing out loud to himself. He stepped forward and knocked again, this time a little harder. He was growing impatient. "Come on, Jimmy," he mumbled to himself. "I'm ready to get this party started. Come on, come on, come on."

Suddenly the door flew open. Jimmy was standing there laughing. "So, you're talkin' to yourself again, huh?" Jimmy cocked his head to the side and smirked. "Hey, y'all!" he turned and yelled into the living room. "Jeffrey's out here talkin' to himself on the front porch!" A burst of laughter rebounded off the walls.

"You know," he said to Jeffrey quietly while peeking his head out the door and looking both ways, "my neighbors are gonna think I got crazy folks comin' to see me if you show up doin' that kinda stuff." Jimmy paused a moment to let the idea sink in. "Man, you know I'm just playin' with you!" he suddenly exclaimed.

"Hey, y'all!" he yelled again into the living room. "Jeffrey thought I was mad at him for talking to himself on the porch!" Another burst of laughter exploded from inside the house. "Come on in, man. You gotta try this fire stuff we got today, son."

"Cool," Jeffrey responded. "Sounds good, but let me chug a beer or two first. You got any liquor?"

"Yep, your favorite…tequila." Jimmy was walking swiftly with a slight limp in his step. He pointed toward the group sitting in his living room and said, "You know all these lame cats already."

"Hey, Jeffrey!" they all yelled out of sync, like an undisciplined barbershop quartet.

"Check out Bobby and Chris over there playing video games," Jimmy resumed, "preparing for who knows what. You'll get no women that way," he sang in a high-pitched voice.

When they reached the kitchen, Jeffrey leaned against one of the counters while Jimmy filled two shotglasses. "You want the lime juice to chase it with?" Jimmy asked.

"Yeah, definitely," Jeffrey replied.

"No problem." Jimmy grabbed the little green plastic bottle off the counter and handed it to Jeffrey. "Here we go. Cheers." They tapped their glasses together, then turned them back.

As Jeffrey forced the tequila down and frantically squirted the lime juice into his mouth, he noticed the scrunched, sour look on Jimmy's face and quickly handed him the bottle of alleviating juice. "You all right, man?" he asked after a second.

"Oh, yeah…now I am," Jimmy answered. "Dang, that one was rough!"

"Congratulations, by the way," Jeffrey said as he placed his shotglass back on the table for a refill.

"Man, I appreciate it," Jimmy said while looking down, setting up two more shots. He raised his head and looked Jeffrey in the eye. "For real, thanks for saying that. I knew you'd be one of the few people to say that and really mean it."

"You're very welcome," Jeffrey replied. "You're not gonna cry, are you? It's too early to be gettin' emotional and all that."

Jimmy laughed and slapped Jeffrey playfully on the shoulder. "Here," he said, handing Jeffrey the shotglass. "Cheers…to good friends…to the best of friends."

"Cheers," Jeffrey echoed. "To best friends and club openings." They clinked their glasses together and downed another dose of the intoxicating poison.

"Sooooo, any girls comin' over later?" Jeffrey suddenly blurted out.

"Man, stop," Jimmy replied. "You already know the answer to that question…but now you've got me wondering. You and Julie break up or something?"

"Nope, everything's good," Jeffrey quickly answered, as if the speedy response would prove his statement to be valid and true. "I might not be able to touch, but I can still look, right?"

"Yeah, I think I've heard that before," Jimmy resumed. "I guess that'll fly…whatever. You ready to try this stuff or what?"

"Oh, yeah!" Jeffrey exclaimed. "Lemme get a beer real quick for when that drainage hits."

"Okay, go ahead." Jimmy slid out of Jeffrey's way and walked to the other side of the kitchen, where the counter was dry. He pulled a quarter ounce of coke from his pocket and started fumbling with the knot at the top of the bag.

"So, you say it's a lot better than what we usually get?"

"Much better…much, much better." Jimmy was untying the sack with fast, shaking hands. "You know how Big Boy always has good stuff, right? Well, this time around it's way better…maybe twice as good. I guess someone down the line forgot to cut it or something…or maybe they just decided to be generous."

He grabbed his license out of his pocket and began shoveling out small amounts from the bag onto the kitchen counter. "Either way, it works out good for us. I'm tellin' you, man… well, you'll see in a second." He took out a dollar bill and laid it on top of the pile and then began rubbing the card back and forth, back and forth, back and forth over the dollar bill.

When he picked up the dollar, the smooth white powder lay flat upon the counter surface like thin linen sheets, like slender plates of gold, like millions of tiny diamonds glistening in the sun. Jimmy broke it down even further by chopping into it with his license, making it finer and finer with each tap of the card upon the counter. Then, he tediously scraped the powder back into a pile, chopped it apart again and scraped it back together, and finally divided it into two lines after swimming in it for nearly a minute. It was obvious he loved the ritual nearly as much as he loved the actual high.

"You wanna go first?" Jimmy asked while rolling up the dollar bill.

"Yeah, lemme see how good this really stuff is," Jeffrey replied, stepping forward to take the dollar bill out of Jimmy's outstretched hand. He approached the kitchen counter quickly, ravenously, but then paused for a second to gaze upon the shiny, sparkling substance, just as pirates gazed upon treasure chests hundreds of years before.

"You gonna snort the line or what?" Jimmy asked.

"Sorry, you know how I cherish these moments, oh, so much," Jeffrey said jokingly. He dipped his head down toward the counter and snorted the line fiercely, voraciously. With eyes closed, he raised his head and sighed in a whistling fashion. His heartbeat suddenly racing, Jeffrey opened his eyes wildly and leaned back on the kitchen counter in an effort to support himself as he smiled triumphantly. He was dazzled.

Jeffrey handed the rolled-up dollar bill back to Jimmy while nodding eagerly with approval. "Dannnnnggggg, you were right. This is some fire stuff."

"Blowed up already, ain't you," Jimmy said as he leaned down over the counter for his chance at bliss. The line of coke stood no chance. He devoured it with one fatal swoop of his nose, and rising victoriously, he looked at Jeffrey with pride and mayhem in his eyes. His look said it all—he loved the fact that he was doing something illegal, something frowned upon by society, something dangerous and troublesome. "Hey, man, you wanna take another shot?" Jimmy asked in a choking voice. "This stuff will make you jittery real quick if you don't watch it."

"Yeah, probably should," Jeffrey responded. "I sure don't wanna start feeling panicky!"

Like a pro, Jimmy hastily filled the shotglasses again. "Cheers, then!" he proclaimed as he handed Jeffrey one glass and held the other close to his chin. "Cheers to…nothing new under the sun."

"Cheers!" Jeffrey shouted in return. *Nothing new under the sun,* Jeffrey repeated to himself silently. *That's a cruel, depressing lie. With one more shot and three more lines, I'm moving ever closer to the place where all things transform into something brand-new under the sun…where everything shines.*

They clinked their glasses together once again and downed the tequila with much more ease than before. This was followed by another shot and then another. Finally, they put down the shotglasses for a rest, considering they might want to slow down a little and just drink beer. To be or not to be slurring, slobbering speech impediments when the girls got there was nothing to ponder over—no paradox—and certainly not a difficult question to answer.

The trick was to balance the coke and the alcohol, to find a happy medium, and everything else—holding decent conversations with beautiful women, making new friends, keeping old friends, coming up with funny jokes on the spot, staying out of fights, getting into fights, driving safely around Atlanta—would fall perfectly into place.

"Come on," Jimmy said. "Let's see what these cats in the living room are doing." They both fired up a Newport and walked swiftly toward the living room. Jeffrey was eager to investigate. While he and Jimmy were talking in the kitchen, he had noticed that shouts interspersed with laughter were constantly bursting into their sanctuary. Because his imagination wasn't willing or able to fill in the blanks, he had to see for himself.

"Boo-yow!" Chris yelled as Jimmy and Jeffrey entered. "Touchdown!" He jumped off the sofa and began doing the Deion Sanders dance while staring at Bobby with beady eyes and laughing intermittently at his frustrated and sad figure. Once he sat back down and regained his peaceful composure, he calmly said to Bobby, "Your game is garbage, man…for real. You should just give up…retire." Everyone in the room burst out laughing.

"Why you gotta be so harsh, man?" Bobby whined.

"Man, I'm just playin' with you…just talkin' crap," Chris replied. "What do you expect? Constructive criticism?" The room was filled with laughter again. "We ain't in no classroom, and I dang sure ain't no teacher or counselor… Jeffrey, tell this man we ain't in no college classroom."

"Nope, no college classroom here," Jeffrey responded. "You're out of luck, Bobby."

"See, what I'd tell you?" Chris was nudging Bobby in the ribs playfully.

"Hold up!" Jimmy suddenly yelled over the chuckles and roars of laughter. "I think I've got a chalkboard in my room!" He leaned over toward Bobby and said in a kind, kindergarten teacher-like voice, "Bobby, would you like for me to get the chalkboard out so Chrissy Poo can draw up some plays and write down some pointers for you?" The room burst into laughter again.

"I hate y'all!" Bobby yelled with fury in his voice. "I'm goin' home! I ain't gotta take this crap from y'all!" He rushed out of the room.

"Awwww, come on," Chris pleaded. "We're just playin' around, man."

"Whatever!" Bobby yelled distantly as he slammed the door behind him.

"Shoot, let 'im go!" Jason suddenly yelled from the corner of the living room. "He's a bum, anyway. He didn't have anything on him and never does. No money, no weed, no dope, no beer." He was counting these things off with a clear display of slowly rising, enormously thick fingers. "He didn't even have any cigarettes! What the heck, man? He just comes around to bum off everybody. I'm tired of that crap! Shoulda beat his butt for slamming the door like that! I say good riddance to the crybaby bum."

"Naw, he's all right, man," Jimmy interrupted. "He has his moments when he's cool to be around…and I have seen him pay for something before…what was it…oh, chewing gum, that was it!"

They all started laughing again. Jimmy had a way of taking the tension out of a room with a quick joke. He also had a way of seeing the best in people. He knew that Bobby wasn't the most favorable company to be around, yet he hung out with him nevertheless…perhaps out of pity. Or perhaps he saw something appealing in his character that no one else saw.

"Alan!" Jason suddenly exclaimed. "Wake up! Let's hit another line."

"Okay," Alan put it simply. Having taken the advice of a wise man who once said "the kindest words are often those not spoken," Alan decided to limit his words to as few as possible. For this reason, he only spoke when it was absolutely necessary—to answer questions, to give advice, to ask a girl out on a date.

"You've got it in your pocket, right?" Jason asked impatiently.

"Yeah," Alan responded.

"Well, get it out, then!" Jason was already holding out his gigantic hand. "I'll chop it up."

Alan quietly handed the sack of coke to Jason, who took it eagerly and hungrily. He had the bag untied and the coke scooped out onto a CD case within seconds.

*Scrape, scrape over the dollar, chop chop with the card—beautiful trails of shining white powder illuminating the plastic surface,* Jeffrey thought as he watched on.

"Is this the same stuff that Jimmy has?" Jeffrey asked curiously.

"Yeah," Jason replied. "Me, Alan, and Jimmy bought a half ounce from Big Boy and then split it down the middle. Alan's holding my part 'cause I always seem to get drunk and lose the sack or jump into a pool with it in my pocket or let some hot girl snort it all."

"How much should I put in on it?" Jeffrey asked.

"Nothing…unless Jimmy wants something for his part," Jason replied.

"You know I don't need any money from you," Jimmy said quickly. "You're all good."

"Yeah, you're no Bobby," Jason continued. "You always put in money, even when you're half broke, so don't worry about it. Consider it our treat tonight."

Jason Thompson braced himself on the arm of the couch in order to move his six-foot-six, three-hundred-pound frame to the floor. Propped up on one knee, he leaned toward the CD case on the coffee table with a cut-off straw in his hand and snorted the line up passionately. He seemed to do everything that way—passionately. With bleeding knuckles and cramping muscles, he had cleared a path on many occasions for Jeffrey to trudge into the end zone during their high school football days.

Now he was using his size and fervor to snatch up, force into submission, and ultimately toss violent drunks from the local bars. Even though his muscles were being rapidly replaced by globs of fat, his loudly slurring, drunken voice could regularly be heard booming above the crowd, "I'll beat the crap out of anybody that tries me. I know that for a fact."

Having witnessed this type of behavior countless times before, and having known about his work history, Jimmy decided to hire him as one of the bouncers at his club. He simply figured that if Jason enjoyed brawling with grown men so much, he should at least be in a position to do it legally and get paid for it.

"Here you go, buddy," Jason said to Alan as he handed him the straw.

Alan was already on his way to the table when he grabbed the straw out of Jason's hand. With his butt barely on the edge of the couch, he stretched toward the table and snorted the line quietly—a quality quite characteristic of him. As a supervisor in his dad's business, he rarely spoke except to give orders and answer questions.

He ate lunch by himself at noon, never uttering a word, just listening intently to the conversation and laughter of the crowd at the other picnic table. However, there was no lack of words for describing Alan Rothman's character. He was first of all loving, then kindhearted, generous, and tranquil. He usually walked around as if he hadn't a worry in the world.

Perhaps it was because he was set to inherit his dad's mining operation in Dahlonega, and therefore, he was set for life. Or maybe his serenity stemmed from his good nature, a nature he diligently worked at day and night. Or…perhaps he was just made that way, and there was no other explanation for it.

Alan turned quickly toward Jimmy and nodded at his hand, which held the cut-off straw, as if to say, *Here, it's your turn.*

"Naw, that straw always cuts the inside of my nose!" Jimmy exclaimed. "I don't see how y'all use it. I got my rolled-up dollar bill right here." He smiled goofily and held it up to his gleaming white teeth as if he was in an ad for a how-best-to-snort-cocaine commercial. Then he maneuvered around the couch and approached the table like he was running in slow motion.

"This is for the gold!" Jimmy stressed. He put the end of the dollar to the CD case and yanked on the line with his nose, producing a loud slurping, sucking sound and nearly bringing the case with him when he rose back up.

"Now, that's how you do it right there, son!" Jimmy yelled with delight as he handed the bill to Chris. "I want my dollar back now," Jimmy said. "I'll be watching you." He looked seriously into Chris's eyes.

Chris couldn't hold up the staring contest for very long and finally broke into laughter at Jimmy's clownish behavior. "You're crazy, man," he said as he turned his attention toward the CD case on the table. Like a concocting shaman or a meditating guru, Chris Jenkins stared at the skinny white line, never taking his eyes off it, as he dropped the PlayStation 3 controller and swooped in for the kill with tremendous focus.

It was his nature to concentrate like that on everything to the nth degree, even when it concerned actions that required little to no thought. From sports to school to sipping coffee on the front porch, this tendency of Chris's hung with him like hyenas upon a vulnerably grounded prey.

While it did prove to be annoyingly insane, it also accounted for his accomplishments in nearly everything he did, especially in the academic field. The combination of natural intelligence and something akin to a monkey on his back had granted Chris a salutatorian status—graduating with a grade point average just slightly lower than Jeffrey's—and a scholarship to study computer science at Georgia Tech.

"Wooooooo-wee! That is some good stuff right there!" Chris proclaimed in a nasally voice.

"Wooooooo-wee?" Jimmy asked with his eyebrows

scrunched together in laughing disbelief. "You sound like you live on a farm or something…like you just finished jumping off your tractor!" Everyone, including Chris, began to laugh.

"Fuuunnnnny man," Chris replied. "Funny, funny man. Is this your new material…breaking out the old knee-slapper jokes? Should I grab a straw hat and start slapping my leg with it while I'm laughing?" Everyone laughed again.

"Do whatcha do," Jimmy responded. "I'm just callin' 'em like I see 'em. However it comes into my head, that's how I shoot it back out."

"That's what I'm talkin' about," Chris resumed. "I swear I'm gonna put you up on a stage one day…maybe be your manager and make oodles of money. Whatcha think about that, Jeffrey?" Chris asked as he extended the rolled-up dollar bill to his friend.

"Sounds like a plan to me," Jeffrey responded, while somewhat reluctantly taking the bill from Chris's hand. He was already beaming from the first line, but he knew that he couldn't neglect his mission. It beckoned him from the distant shores across oceans of despair.

Like a lighthouse desperately signaling lost and fearful souls, it drew him in with an overwhelmingly intense luminosity that blinded him from everything else in his life until his spirit tingled with pure joy and childlike anticipation. He cherished the moment until the vision ran dry, then he stooped down to rejoin what he saw to be his soulmate waiting patiently upon the shores of a newly discovered world.

"What'd I tell y'all!" Jimmy suddenly exclaimed. "Jeffrey would for real marry this stuff if he could!" Jeffrey barely avoided laughing and blowing the coke off the case.

"I see what you're sayin' now," Jason said. "Man, I thought

I loved doing this stuff, but I ain't got nothin' on Jeffrey. Did you see that glare in his eyes? I thought he was gonna go Cujo on us and start foaming at the mouth. What the heck, man?"

Jeffrey shrugged his shoulders as if to simply say that's just the way it is, but he knew it was more than that, much more than that, something he could never put into words. So he left it at that—with an insufficient shrug of his shoulders.

For the next hour or so, the living room was hazy with smoke and laughter, saturated with yelling and alcohol, and smothered with cocaine and deep conversation. Jimmy felt like he was on the outside looking in through a camera lens at strange figures who moved fast-forwardly before slowing to a halt, only to jolt up once again and vibrate erratically in their seats.

Jeffrey was at the center of it all, gratefully absorbing every moment as the group bragged about girlfriends, imitated their favorite Dave Chappelle sayings, argued whether or not Bruce Lee was the best fighter in the history of the world, discussed why it was better to snort cocaine out of piles rather than lines, and rated the hottest actresses.

As evening arrived, the boys' minds were still flooded with fervor, but the laughter and yelling had dropped off as the conversations took a deeper and darker turn toward more serious subjects. As soon as Jimmy heard the words "ancient aliens," he carefully and discreetly slipped out of the room, blew a sigh of relief in the hallway, and entered his bedroom to do more practical things.

He had heard these in-depth conversations way too many times, especially when Jeffrey and Chris were around. Nevertheless, the living room party continued on in a paradoxical blending of mind-numbing drugs and intellectual conversation. Black holes, the Big Bang theory, UFOs, USOs, and the December 21st, 2012 end of Mayan calendar dominated the space-time curvature separating the relative IQs of the various participants.

Jason found himself empty of both words and thoughts. Finally, a subject he could connect with arose like a plume of smoke in the sky—the necessary and extraordinarily destructive action of dropping a nuclear weapon on various terrorist-laden countries.

"I don't think we'll ever do it," Chris said. "Too much public opinion against everything. Too many idiots running their mouths, crying about ten people dying in a war. It's a war, for goodness' sake!"

"Or they whine about us killing innocent civilians," Jason piped in. "Who is innocent in an area that harbors terrorists? Are they pointing out the terrorists to us? No! They dress and act just like the terrorists because…let's face it…they support them. The devil's religion, if you ask me. Somebody should turn that desert into a glass parking lot. Israel will do it if all these other girls are too shaky in their boots!"

"That's insane," Jeffrey said. "Most, if not all of it."

"That's right," Jason replied. "Insane is what we might want to be if we want to win. They seem pretty insane themselves."

Suddenly, the imaginary violence ceased, as a resounding gong exploded forth at the end of the hallway, vibrating the walls of the house as it traveled from one bedroom to the next, into and out of the bathroom, down the remainder of the hallway, and into the kitchen.

When it finally reached the living room, the sound seemed to have been amplified ten times over, as if the house was custom-built to perform as a modern-day speaker box or an ancient Roman amphitheater, boosting the sound by reducing interference patterns, resonant frequencies, diffraction, and standing wave energy.

With a look of bewilderment, Jeffrey said, "This house must be some sort of acoustical wonder."

"Yeah, it is!" Chris responded as he looked confusingly at the walls and the ceiling. "That is weird."

The gong resounded again, ostensibly louder than before. The four young men in the living room were all squinting at each other with a what-in-the-world-is-going-on look of dis-array.

"Whatever it is, it's very annoying!" Jason yelled over the fading echoes of the last gong.

After the vibrations had ceased, the confusion remained. They all looked at one another with quizzical eyes that begged the question: *Why does it feel like we're in some sort of castle or haunted house?*

"How do y'all like my new doorbell?" Jimmy suddenly asked as he crossed the room. "By the confused look on all your faces, I can tell you think that crap is cool." He nodded and smiled.

"Has he lost his mind?" Chris whispered to Jeffrey.

"If he hasn't, then I've lost mine," Jeffrey responded. "Who buys an *Addams Family*–sounding doorbell? That's some of the most off-the-wall crap I've ever heard of."

"Who's that, the girls?" Jason yelled across the room.

"Nope, even better!" Jimmy yelled back. "Well, depending on your definition of fun and how long it's been since you had a girlfriend! Pills, baby, pills!"

When Jimmy opened the door, the friendliest looking, cleanest-cut white boy was slightly bouncing back and forth on the front porch, as if he were in a rush but with nowhere to go. He had on a navy-blue Polo shirt with a matching white and blue baseball cap, and blue jeans that were heavily weighed down in the pockets by bags and bags of pills. "Whatcha up to, man?" he asked.

"Not much," Jimmy replied. "My club opens tonight… otherwise, just gettin' high. Come on, let's go in the kitchen."

"What do we need pills for?" Jason asked after Jimmy and his friend disappeared through the doorway.

"Man, you can always take pills," Jeffrey responded instantly. "They go with everything…alcohol, coke, whatever."

"That's on y'all, then," Jason returned. "I think I'll just stick to the two chemicals I got working right now—my beer and my blow." He took a big swig out of the bottle in his hand and then resumed. "Y'all need to be careful popping pills. I had this one friend who almost died because he mixed…what were those pills he took?" Jason was lost in thought for a moment. "Oh, yeah! Methadone and Xanax, that's what they were. He had just got through doing a keg stand and then he—"

With their swift passage through the doorway and back into the living room, Jimmy and the preppy white boy interrupted Jason's boring lecture about the safety precautions to take when mixing prescription drugs. Silence ensued until the boy nervously vibrated back out into the Atlanta air and the door closed with a *boom* and a *click*.

"Who was that?" Jason asked as soon as the door was closed.

"Don't worry about all that," Jimmy replied. "He's just a little shady because he takes a ton of pills and gets blitzed out of his mind. We can't all be socialites like you, Jason." Everyone laughed at Jason's expense.

"Ha, ha, ha," Jason mockingly repeated. "Very fu—"

"So, what kinda pills did you get?" Jeffrey interrupted.

"Five rolls and ten forty-milligram Oxycontins," Jimmy replied proudly.

"That's what I'm talkin' about," Jeffrey said hungrily.

"Okay, y'all!" Jimmy's booming voice brought everyone's thoughts and actions to a halt. "Come up one by one and get your pills. I got a roll and two oxycontins for everyone. Jason, if you don't want yours, I'll take 'em…or split 'em with Jeffrey."

"That's cool with me!" Jason shouted across the room.

"Single file now, single file," Jimmy resumed.

As soon as Jeffrey washed the pills down with a yank on his bottle, he had the strong feeling he had forgotten something. He checked his pockets for his keys, his money, his lighter, his cigarettes, his cell phone—everything seemed perfectly intact. He was ready to go, but this feeling was trying to pull him back.

This was something that occurred frequently to Jeffrey when all of a sudden he thought, *I had a date with Julie tonight. Dang, man. That's what I forgot. Oh, well. Just gotta blow it off now, forget about it. Dismiss my subconscious and unconscious thoughts butting in, getting in the way.*

"All right, everybody!" Jimmy yelled again. "We gotta go! Grab your coke sacks and a beer or two for the road! I'm driving! Oh, and please, *please* don't talk about aliens or nuclear warfare when we get around these girls who we're meeting up with! Please, don't let 'em do it!" he pleaded loudly with his face toward the sky. "Please, don't let 'em do it!" Everyone laughed, promised to be cool, then laughed again while Jimmy continuously moaned into the heavens, "Please…don't…let 'em…do it!"

# ❧ 10 ❧

The blue neon sign screamed radiantly across the parking lot and into the street with a Seinfeld–Kenny Roger's–Roasters brightness. From the street to the door, Jeffrey shielded his hallucinating eyes from the blinding flood of light. "Dang, that junk is bright!" he exclaimed to Jimmy as they finally reached the sidewalk. "People will be able to see that crap from the interstate, man!" Jeffrey squinted and blinked a few times to ensure that his eyes were working properly.

"That's the plan," Jimmy responded. "Nobody can say they don't know about my club. They'll see that freaking bright neon sign from here to Dahlonega. And then they'll get curious, exit the interstate, drive down this street, park in this parking lot, and walk up here, just like we did. And, *bam*, this is what they'll see!" Jimmy winked at the bouncer standing nearby, then slung the doors open wide.

Jeffrey was astonished. From the plainly decorated stage to the dark, wooden bars to the small circular tables and chairs, the place was a perfect replica of the blues clubs he had seen in old pictures and movies, even down to the characters in the crowd. Men and women yelled into deafened ears, the alcohol exploding loudly from their breath.

Cigarettes burned and sizzled, emitting smoke that rose discreetly, curled upon reaching the ceiling, and slithered around the low-hanging lights. People juked and jived, squirmed and sprinted to snag lucrative positions at the various bars. Jeffrey stood frozen like a child in a museum, devouring every detail with wild, hungry eyes.

He loved to witness the age-old American tradition of alcoholism in its truest and simplest form. As he studied the obscure sadness on the Piano Man faces in the crowd, Jeffrey recognized the destructive nature of the serpentine sauce. He saw wives throw away marriages like common garbage as they danced without inhibition on the hard, slick floors. He saw husbands leave starving families at home while they gulped down tall, icy mugs of golden bliss. He saw college students light their futures ablaze while they cheered and threw back shotglasses of multicolored poisons.

He saw young, working men and women looking for love and happiness in the magical concoctions of modern-day sorcerers. The sorrow-ridden figures were worlds apart in life, and yet all the same, possessed by a fiery desire to suddenly lose the control they struggled so hard to grasp, obsessed with the love of finding oblivion in a conscious state, infatuated with the lies and self-deception that were slowly drowning their souls.

They could have reached the truth so easily if they had only—the loudness that overcame the self-reflection-bringing silence was offered in a simple little glass, easy to acquire and even easier to consume.

*Then again,* Jeffrey thought, *who's worried about self-destruction or alcoholism? These people might have figured it all out. Is life really all that great? Should we drag it on and on like a giant yoke on our backs? Better to use, come out of our shells, feel the music flow with the buzz, shout because we have something seemingly important to say, and ruin our health so we can rest sooner.*

*Besides,* Jeffrey's thoughts continued, *there's just something so poetic in a man slowly bringing about his own destruction, especially if his deceivingly bright, shiny crutch reveals its failing bolts and faulty pins for all the world to see.*

"So, what do y'all think?" Jimmy yelled as he turned to face his friends.

Words like *nice*, *cool*, and *awesome* bombarded him. From their excited faces and the tone of their voices, Jimmy knew his friends were not simply flattering him. He turned back toward the crowd, looked at the stage for a moment, then smiled with relief. His club would be a success. He could feel it in his bones. The plunge was no longer a pipe dream, and he no longer had to convince himself that his *eureka* moment was realistic. This was concrete evidence, words etched in stone.

"Come on, y'all!" Jimmy yelled back at them. "I've got us a special table set up off to the side up here!"

It was nearly impossible to hear over the music, but Jimmy's voice, as usual, seemed to override and reduce every secondary noise in the vicinity. Alan, Jason, Chris, and Jeffrey followed giddily behind as Jimmy nudged forward, opening a tiny pathway through the tightly compressed crowd. When they reached the table, five tall mugs of beer were waiting on them, resting on flimsy coasters, sweating down their sides as if they had sprinted ahead so they could give the young men a warm welcome.

"Hey, Jimmy!" shouted a cute, young brunette standing beside the black table and the sparkling, golden mugs. "Do you need anything else?"

"No, I think we're—"

"Lemme get ten shots of Crown Royal!" Jeffrey interrupted.

Everyone at the table looked at him with odd, squinting

eyes. Jeffrey gritted his teeth and licked his lips rapidly before answering their stares. "Don't worry, I'm buying! If you don't want yours, I'll drink it for you!" He was already in a state of mad pleasure, but something inside kept pushing him. *Go on!* Jeffrey thought. *Until you're completely saturated by all of it.*

"Okay, ten shots of Crown," the waitress mumbled for her own benefit as she wrote the order down on a small notepad. "Anything else?"

"No, I think that'll be all, Monica!" Jimmy yelled before looking over at Jeffrey to make sure he wasn't about to shout out another round of drinks. "Thank you, baby!"

As she walked away, Jeffrey, Chris, Jason, and Alan all twisted and strained their necks, trying to absorb every detail of her skirt, her legs, her long-flowing hair before she disappeared into the crowd. Jimmy did no such thing. Instead, he slowly leaned over toward the center of the table and said, "Kissed her…last Tuesday, I think…yeah, Tuesday."

With pangs of jealousy throbbing in his chest, Jason shook his head and yelled, "You're a lucky man!"

"Oh, no, no, no," Jimmy replied, still leaning on the table with a cocky grin. "You are mistaken. Luck ain't got nothin' to do with it."

"Well…what is it, then?" Jason inquired.

"That's something you'll have to learn on your own someday, son," Jimmy replied sarcastically as if he was sitting on the bedside, tucking Jason in for the night.

"Well, that's just greatttt!" Jason resumed in a frustrating tone.

"Y'all look at this man over here trying to get pointers on how to get a girl!" Jeffrey burst forth. Again, at Jason's expense, everyone cracked up laughing.

Seeing the redness grow fuller and fuller in Jason's face, Jimmy blurted out the first thing that came to mind, "Okay, I will tell you one thing, the most important and most basic thing…you ready?" After receiving no response, Jimmy continued anyway, "You gotta be nice to 'em. Plain and simple. Tell 'em they're pretty, their hair smells good, their feet look cute in those shoes, whatever. Oh, and compliment their eyes, definitely compliment their eyes. They eat that up. You can practice tonight when these girls show up…if they ever get here."

"Or ask Jeffrey!" Chris piped in. "Lord knows what he must have said or done to get a girl like Julie! I'll be danged if he's not experimenting with some voodoo or a Ouija board!" Everyone cracked up again, with Jason laughing the loudest.

Jeffrey smiled and laughed with the others until it struck him that he had forgotten about Julie. "Oh, crap!" he said, panic rippling through his gut.

"What?" Chris asked, trying to look concerned.

"I forgot about Julie," Jeffrey replied with a drooping jaw. "We were supposed to do something tonight."

"You never did call her after you talked to me?" Jimmy asked inquisitively.

"Nope, I was in too much of a rush to get to your house… and then…dang!" Jeffrey tried to remember if he'd even thought about calling her during those perfect windows of opportunity—riding on the MARTA, walking to Jimmy's, the entire time he was snorting, drinking, laughing, talking. *Why did I never think about calling her?* Jeffrey wondered.

"Uhhhh-ohhhh!" Jason said mockingly. "Jeffrey's gonna be in trouuuble!"

"You need to go ahead and call her now," Jimmy advised. "At least that way you don't leave her hanging all night, worrying, wondering what happened to you."

"Man, she's gonna be pissed!" Jeffrey lowered his head and stared at the table.

"So what!" Jimmy resumed. "She'll be even madder tomorrow. I'm tellin' you, you need to call her now and get it over with. I think she'll live. She'll be all right by tomorrow."

"You don't understand," Jeffrey opened up. "She'll be all over me about where I am, what I'm doing! I'll just call her tomorrow."

"Okay, it's your grave, buddy," Jimmy said consolingly.

*No fear of graves*, Jeffrey pondered. *What a buzzkill that conversation would be. I won't be dragged down, not right now.*

"Where are those shots?" Jeffrey blurted out. "I feel like I need one right about now…maybe two."

"She'll be here in a minute, Jeffrey." Jimmy spoke quickly and turned his head toward the stage. "I think they're about to start. You hear that?"

There was some clattering backstage. It sounded as if the drummer was dragging his equipment across the floor. For nearly a minute, a swift, angry voice lashed out at the scraping and the banging until, finally, even the crowd grew silent. Everyone had their eyes on the stage. In wonderment, they looked as if some mysterious force was causing all of this commotion and was about to reveal itself. Slowly, the curtains pulled back, and the lights glared into the crowd.

Jimmy squinted his eyes for a moment while his pupils adjusted to the lights shouting from the stage. When he could finally make out the figures, he saw two elderly men in black, double-breasted suits with serious, dark faces. They were geared up and ready to play. The frontman rested his right hand on the guitar strapped around his neck and grabbed the microphone with his left.

"My name is Willy Johnson," the blues guitarist and singer said. "And this is my brother, Rufus." He turned and pointed toward the drums. Rufus raised his hand, as if to say he was present but never squeaked a word or a smile. Willie nodded at his brother and turned to face the crowd again. "We are the Blues Brothers," he said with a deep, scratchy voice.

As if to build suspense, he neither uttered another word, nor moved a single muscle for the next fifteen seconds. He just stared at the crowd, perhaps waiting for them to offer up their inhibitions, to sacrifice themselves to the music that he and his brother were about to play. Then he slowly began to pluck the strings of his guitar.

Once the timing felt right, his brother joined in with a moderate beat. Willy suddenly moaned, "The thrill is gone… the thrill is gone away." The crowd roared for a second before coming to a standstill again. Jeffrey nearly broke his neck turning to yell at the waitress, who was now standing still watching the stage. Jason whispered something to Alan before they both popped up and rushed to the bathroom to hit a bump of coke in the stalls. Chris continued to yell and clap as if the first few words from Willy were continuously resonating in his head.

But Jimmy…Jimmy did something very different from everyone else. He wasn't worried about drinks or coke or yelling or clapping or any other external distraction. He simply closed his eyes and absorbed the music that vibrated through the air. He unconsciously assumed a painfully empty expression as Willy's words and woes soaked into his soul. This experience transcended the club, the drugs, the money, the women, everything. He would have never acknowledged it, but Jimmy knew that he possessed something rare and priceless.

Meanwhile, Jeffrey was looking for the same type of transcendence in the bottom of a shotglass. When the waitress finally arrived, Jeffrey already had money in hand and was barely able to say "keep the change" before one of the glasses hit his lips. There was not even the hint of a grimace on his face as he swiftly clinked the shotglass down onto the table and picked up another one.

To Chris and Jimmy's amazement, he downed that one too, and then another, without even pausing to look up or chase the liquor with his beer. "Let's hit a line or a bump or something," Jeffrey said at the end of his clinic on binge drinking. "Or just give me a decent-sized rock, and I'll shoot it up my nose."

"All right, man…just slow down." Jimmy was no longer transcending. He pulled out the glowing white sack and started to untie it.

"You're gonna do it right here?" Jeffrey asked.

"Yeah!" Jimmy responded. "Why not? I own this place! I'm gonna lay lines down right on the edge of this table."

"For real?" Chris asked in a semi-high-pitched voice.

"For real, for real," Jimmy resumed. "Naw, but you might wanna ease that way in your seat a little bit, Jeffrey. That way you sort of block everyone's view. We don't want all these people to see us doin' this."

*Beautiful white powder glistening on the glossy black tabletop, waiting for us all to give in to its beauty*, Jeffrey thought. *So it can hook us good and direct our paths into the Valley of the Shadow of Death. With bits in our mouths and Death riding on our backs, we will be like horses running this way and that, according to the commands of our Fuhrer.*

"Jeffrey, stop daydreaming and hit your line already!" Jimmy shouted from the outside world.

"Oh, y'all have already gone?" Jeffrey asked.

"Yeah, come on!" Jimmy was holding up a loosely rolled dollar bill.

Jeffrey snatched it from his hand like a wild man ready to leap into that valley and slung his head down as if he were going for the bit. He found his Fuhrer at the edge of the black, glossy table in Jimmy's Blues that night around nine o'clock. One of the most important moments of Jeffrey's life—his ritualistic passing from recreation to addiction—was just as invisible as the rhythm and blues that filled the air.

There was no feeling of anxiety, sadness, or remorse. There was no *eureka* moment. There was only the familiar ecstasy that accompanied every line he had ever snorted. Just as the girls were showing up and the party was really kicking off, Jeffrey was unknowingly entering a labyrinth from which there was no escape.

"Look at these beautiful girls here!" Jimmy shouted. "Y'all take a seat wherever you want or right by me if you like."

As if prearranged, the four girls split in the middle, seating themselves two on each side of the semicircular booth, squeezing and sliding their rear ends along the leather cushions.

"So good to see y'all," Jimmy said with a polished smile and a charming tone. He paused for a moment to appreciate each one of them for their particular, dazzling qualities. "Oh, where are my manners?" he suddenly proclaimed. "Chris, Jeffrey, this is Ashley, Beth, Kathy, and Anita…Ashley, Beth, Kathy, Anita, this is Chris and Jeffrey. Jason and Alan must be hiding out somewhere or got lost or something."

"Why are there only four girls, man?" Jeffrey whispered to Jimmy as they found themselves sitting next to one another.

"Because you've got a girlfriend, Jeffrey boy," Jimmy whispered back. "You know I do a lot of stuff and bend a lot of… rules, I guess, but that's one thing I don't mess with—people's relationships. I mean, I don't think Julie's the one or a saint or anything like that, but I still don't want to be the one responsible or semi-responsible for y'all breaking up. You might hold it against me one day, even if you don't know you're holding it against me."

"I understand completely," Jeffrey resumed. "I'm not gonna argue with you on that point, not for a second. I appreciate you lookin' out for me, man. Oh! Here come the sneaky boys now!"

Jason and Alan slid alongside the crowd, laughing and nudging each other about some smart remark Jason had made to another guy in the bathroom. It appeared they wouldn't make it to the table without stumbling terribly or falling face first on the floor. When they finally looked up and saw the girls sitting at the table, they became as straight as boards. Jason froze for a moment, and in that moment, his composure was destroyed.

When he started to walk again, it looked as if someone had cut his Achilles' tendons or ripped out the ligaments in his knees. Alan, on the other hand, used this moment to mysteriously transform into an overconfident, slick, charming young man. As if some secret switch had been flipped on the inside of his head, he unconsciously converted his sloppy, awkward steps into a stroll with a slight hitch that was as smooth as crystalline glass.

Alan made it to the table first, nodded his head with confidence, winked at one of the girls, then slid into the booth next to another. Jason slowly approached and acted confused as to where he was supposed to sit. "Right there across from me," Alan said, pointing more at the girl than at the open seat next to her.

"Dang, I gotta do this junk again!" Jimmy yelled. He took a deep breath and then quickly said, "Alan, Jason, this is Ashley, Beth, Kathy, and Anita…Ashley, Beth, Kathy, Anita, this is Alan and Jason. Y'all have fun with that."

When Jeffrey looked over, Ashley was whispering something into Jimmy's ear. He already knew exactly what she was saying. Jimmy's hand quickly reached for his right pocket, where he was holding his powder.

When Alan and Chris saw this, they followed suit. With three sacks out on the table, there was nearly enough powder to invite the next table or two over. Pretty soon, the coke was cut neatly into three different sections of three lines each—monstrous lines. Straws and dollar bills passed back and forth like clockwork until there was nothing left but three circles of faint, white mist on the table.

Jeffrey yelled for the waitress again, Alan slid a little closer to Beth and whispered something in her ear, Chris cocked his head back and laughed exuberantly at something Kathy had said, Jason sat still like a stone, uncomfortably glancing over at Anita every once in a while, and Jimmy leaned back with his arm around Ashley, pulling her a little closer as he smiled slyly. Everyone seemed to be having a great time except for Jeffrey and Jason. They were both antsy, one because he had a girl beside him and the other because he did not.

"Hey, baby!" Jeffrey yelled out as the pretty, brown-haired girl approached the table. "Can we get nine shots, five beers, and four margaritas, please?"

"Yeah, sweetcheeks!" she replied. "What kind of shots?"

"Ummm…I think we'll go with tequila this time…Cuervo Gold!" Jeffrey gazed across the table to make sure no one had any complaints.

"Okay, I gotcha, baby!" the waitress resumed.

"No, you ain't got me yet, but you can…any time!" Jeffrey shouted as he performed some type of odd, grossly overkilled wink.

"Oh…okay!" the slim beauty shouted as she scrunched her eyebrows together and awkwardly walked away.

Jeffrey nudged Jimmy in the ribs and yelled, "What did I just say to that girl? 'You ain't got me yet, but you can? Any time?"

Jimmy had already been quietly chuckling to himself, and he now burst out laughing as he nodded his head up and down. "Oh, man!" he said in a high-pitched voice. "That's some of the jivest crap…" Suddenly, Jimmy turned his head to the rest of the people at the table. He was laughing so hard that he nearly knocked the table over as he rapidly bounced up and down and rocked back and forth in the booth. Everyone stared at him, wondering what was going on, until he finally squeezed out the words, "Did y'all hear what Jeffrey just said to our waitress?"

"No," Chris answered for the crowd. "What did he say, something crazy?"

Jimmy laughed hard for another ten or twenty seconds before he regained his composure enough to yell, "After the waitress said, 'I gotcha, baby…'" Suddenly, Jimmy was rocking back and forth, laughing again. He looked up at the ceiling and took a deep breath before finishing: "This man said, 'You ain't got me yet, but you can…any time!'" The table roared with laughter, but no one was laughing louder than Jimmy and Jeffrey!

"I winked at her real hard after I said it too!" Jeffrey yelled.

Jimmy's high-pitched "Oh, man!" was barely audible over

the ever-increasing roar of laughter that could now fill almost half of the club.

Once the hilarity of the moment had ended and all the cackling had died down, Jimmy leaned over to Jeffrey and said, "Sorry to bust you out like that, man, but that stuff was just too funny to keep to myself."

"Man, you know I don't get embarrassed about stuff like that," Jeffrey responded, chuckling again. "If anything, it's funny when I royally bomb. In fact, I think it's better because now I can only go up. I mean, I can't say anything worse or more lame, right?"

"You're right about that!" Jimmy returned. "You surely can't say anything more jive to that girl, but I don't know if that puts you in a better position to hook up with her, like you think it does. Your theory may be a little skewed on that note."

"I don't know, we'll see." Jeffrey looked as if he was lost in thought, blocking everything out for the time being in order to run back over his royal bomb theory. After a few seconds, he just shook his head. Obviously, it wasn't worth contemplating; it would just have to be played out in real time like an experiment in a laboratory.

"Just out of curiosity," Jimmy continued, "did you say something like that the first time you met Julie?"

"I don't know…I doubt it." Jeffrey looked puzzled, as if he couldn't remember the first time he met Julie. "Anyway, on a different note, I wanna pay for the drinks that I'm ordering tonight. I know you'll probably say they're on the house or they're free at the end, but for real, let me pay for 'em. I'm here to help your business prosper, not plummet."

"Man, I appreciate that," Jimmy replied. "You don't know how much…and yes, I was gonna put the drinks on the house, but I'll let you pay since you insist."

Jimmy shifted back toward Ashley. As he put his arm around her again, he was thinking what a good friend he had in Jeffrey. "Hey, baby," he whispered in her ear, "listen to what they're about to play next. They're gonna switch up to something a little more romantic, some Otis Redding." Almost in perfect unison with Willy on the stage, Jimmy started gently singing in her ear, "These arms of mine, they are lonely."

She looked up at him and smiled beautifully before giggling a tiny bit and snuggling up a little closer under his arm. Jimmy turned and winked at Jeffrey, as if to say *Here's how you really run game on the girls."* Jeffrey simply smiled and shook his head a little in admiration before wrenching his neck around to spot the waitress at the bar. She was coming his way.

"All right, I can't believe I was able to get all of this on one tray," said the beautifully bouncing girl. She placed the tray down gently and began handing out drinks. When she got to Jeffrey, he said, "Thank you very much."

"You are very welcome," she responded before giving him a sweet, kind smile.

After she moved on to the other parties at the table, Jeffrey nudged Jimmy in the ribs and said, "See, I'm moving up already…not jive at all."

"Yeah, not too shabby," Jimmy responded without adding *"but not too impressive either."*

"What'd I tell you?" Jeffrey resumed. "Nowhere to go but up…and did you see that sweet smile she gave me?"

"Yep, very sweet." Jimmy pursed his lips and nodded his head up and down. "Very, very sweet."

"Soooo, ya need anything else?" asked the perfume-wearing, perfectly tanned girl.

"No, I don't think so," Jeffrey responded. "Thanks, baby."

The girl's cheeks turned a little red, but it was difficult to tell if she was blushing because of the flirtation or holding back an enormous laugh because of the earlier pickup line. Jeffrey would never know for sure. She turned around and walked away without another word.

Assuming she was blushing under those exquisitely long eyelashes, Jeffrey faced everyone at the table with a strong, confident smile. "Cheers!" he yelled, picking up his shotglass. "To Jimmy's Blues!"

"To Jimmy's Blues!" everyone shouted before clinking their glasses together at the center of the table, downing the tequila, and desperately reaching for their limes.

The glasses of beer and mixed drinks, the shots of liquor, the off-the-wall, irrelevant cheers, the combination of cackling, snickering, and giggling, the flirtatious acts from both sexes, and the lines—the beautiful white lines—all promenaded around the hazy, smoke-filled booth for another hour or so. More and more, it seemed to Jeffrey as if they were all closed off from the rest of the people in the club, as if the atmosphere on their planet was always like a day at the beach where the horizon bursts with multiple suns.

Suddenly, Jason furiously shouted, "What the what, man!" to a well-dressed man who had accidentally spilled half his beer in Jason's lap. Jeffrey snapped his head around, ready to pummel the jerk who had ticked off his friend and ended his own captivating daydream. They rose simultaneously, Jason to get in the face of the hotheaded, rich boy, and Jeffrey to hurdle the back of the booth. Within an instant, they were both pointing their fingers feverishly, only inches away from the man's forehead.

"You spilt your drink in my lap, you idiot!" Jason raged as

he shuffled closer and closer to the coat and tie-wearing executive.

The cocky, Wall Street–looking man smiled and swaggered as if he were untouchable, like money or a higher social status would protect him from renegades like the violent-eyed men before him.

Overcome with anger, Jeffrey swung without warning, attempting to rip the smug look off the arrogant man's face. His right hook landed squarely on the man's jaw, causing his eyes to go blank and his body to go limp. Despite the fact that he was already on his way to the ground, Jason followed swiftly with a haymaker that nearly crushed the man's nose and sent him crashing even faster into the hard, concrete floor.

There was no need for any rib kicking or face smashing once the poor executive had hit the floor. Jason and Jeffrey's point had been proven and enough damage had been done—Mr. Wall Street wouldn't be getting up anytime soon.

"Dannnnnggggg, y'all knocked him out cold!" Jimmy yelled from the back of the booth. He had been standing on the seat cushion watching the whole thing.

"Heck, yeah!" Jason responded, turning his head quickly. "All he had to do was apologize, that's it! Instead, he gives me and Jeffrey this cocky look like he's better than us." Jason turned back toward the body on the floor. "You stupid, arrogant moron!" he yelled as the blood continued to rush through his eyes.

"I think I might have hit him anyway, apology or not!" Jeffrey said with a laugh as he looked at Jimmy, then back at Jason.

Suddenly, the crowd split down the middle as two bouncers rushed toward the scene. They looked angry and intense at first, ready to snatch someone up and throw him out on his butt, until they recognized Jason and then saw Jimmy standing and smiling in the booth behind him.

"What happened, man? This dude's out cold," the first bouncer said as he gave Jason a somewhat surprised and horrified look.

"He was talking crap, so me and my friend decked him," Jason responded.

"Oh, well, I guess that's what he gets!" the second bouncer exclaimed in an excited fashion. "Nothin' but an Italian shoe-wearing rich boy, anyway. Come on, let's get 'em out of here."

They picked him up by his feet and hands and began to carry him slowly through the crowd. "Oh, Jimmy!" the first bouncer shouted out. "Come 'ere real quick!"

"Yeah, what's up?" Jimmy inquired as he approached.

"Since the man's knocked out like this," the bouncer explained, "you know we'll have to call the cops and probably the paramedics, so—"

"Yeah, I gotcha," Jimmy interrupted, already assuming what he was going to say next. "We'll go ahead and leave. Just tell 'em it was some gangbangers that jumped the guy and then ran."

"Sounds good to me," the bouncer replied. "Sorry about y'all having to leave."

"That's all right," Jimmy returned. "I've seen all I needed to see tonight. Thanks for your help."

"No problem, Mr. Weathers," the bouncers said in unison.

"My father is Mr. Weathers…just call me Jimmy," he said as he slightly lifted his hand to indicate that he was saying good-bye. "Y'all have a good night."

The group left the club and headed to Jimmy's house, most

of them hoping to regain the utopian atmosphere that they'd easily erected before the brawl had tainted the night with savagery. Leading the way, Jeffrey and Jason strutted across the street reenacting the event and praising one another's triumph like warriors returning home from battle or heavyweight champions of the world celebrating their still-undefeated record.

Alan, Beth, Chris, Kathy, and Anita followed them at a short distance, swaying as if controlled by the whims and impulsiveness of the wind, laughing at their inability to coordinate their steps appropriately. Jimmy and Ashley lagged way behind. They were walking hand in hand, talking, laughing, and occasionally staring at one another with wonder-filled eyes.

Once they got back to Jimmy's, making out seemed like the ideal nightcap, but only after most of the drugs and alcohol were gone, of course. For Jeffrey, there was no such thing as a nightcap. He planned on staying awake for as long as his body and his money could hold out, even if it meant cutting class for a few days and avoiding or possibly even involving Julie in his spontaneous bender.

The future didn't really matter—plans, outlines, deadlines, all was meaningless at the moment—because his mind could only focus on the beautiful white lines streaking like the smoke from airplanes high in the sky.

# 11

After what seemed like a few weeks to Jeffrey, a month and a half had passed by. He and Jimmy were now becoming troublesome, unknowingly bringing trouble upon themselves. They banged on their friends' doors at odd times during the night and early into the morning, they cussed out drug dealers for falling asleep, they dodged police officers even when their pockets were dry, they spent money as if they were shoveling it into a bonfire, and they roamed the streets nearly every night looking for something sinister and dangerous to get into.

Over this short time period, Jeffrey was forced to drop all of his classes for fear of flunking out, and he had broken things off with Julie because of her ridiculous, high-maintenance demands and her constant nagging about drugs, alcohol, and the ruination of his life. Meanwhile, Jimmy's business was rapidly circling the bowl, growing ever closer to the dismal drain at the end.

Despite the obvious mental fatigue and looming infrastructural collapse around them, Jimmy and Jeffrey continued to fly down this road, a road they had paved just for themselves for their own destruction. It was poorly constructed, awkwardly designed, and erratically organized, but somehow it retained some aspect of the sublime.

As long as Jimmy and Jeffrey kept their eyes off the unstable ground beneath them, they could continue to build and build and build…forever, it seemed. If not for the mysterious and awe-inspiring lights along the slippery street, the superhighway would collapse in upon itself like a massive, aging star whose core ceases to generate energy.

During this destructive timespan, Jeffrey remained convinced he could fix it all in a moment whenever he wished, that the quicksand enveloping him could never drown a man of such fortitude and supernatural strength. In some sense, he was right. If he jumped out of the car before everything collapsed, he could salvage his relationship with Julie. She would embrace him simply because he had quit drinking and drugging. She would rejoice in the fact that she had been proven right, that the drugs and alcohol were the things clouding his judgment and destroying his life.

Then, when the moment felt right, Jeffrey would promise to be a more responsible, sober person. He had seen similar situations in movies a hundred times or more, and things always worked out in the end. As for school, he had merely missed a semester, just as if he were extremely ill or had personal problems with his family. It was no big deal. Though he might lose his scholarship, he could still continue to get financial aid, and apply for the Pell Grant. Besides, he hadn't hurt his GPA or lost any mental faculties—those were the most important things.

Nearly a month later, Jimmy and Jeffrey were forced to glance at the cavern beneath both sides of their ever-narrowing road. They had been up for days on a real bender, chasing coke, oxycontin, and demerol with pint after pint of liquor. Jimmy's old girlfriend, Molly, had been calling him around the clock, talking about getting back together, so he and Jeffrey were making a road trip back to their hometown of Dahlonega.

Jimmy couldn't be more excited. This was his chance to get

her back. Molly had broken up with him right after high school for some reason he couldn't remember. *But all that is irrelevant*, Jimmy thought. *She wants to get back together with me.*

They were just entering Dahlonega when Jimmy received the news that would ultimately deal him his fatal blow. Molly called to say that their rendezvous was off, that her old boyfriend, after finally realizing how important and special she was, had popped up unexpectedly with a huge diamond ring. Jimmy didn't wait to hear any further explanation or pathetic apology. He dropped the phone into the floorboard and slowly pulled over to the side of the road.

From Jimmy's reaction and the few words he picked up during the conversation, Jeffrey knew precisely what had happened. He wanted to say, *"Man, forget that girl! Let's go home."* But he thought that might be inappropriate at the moment, and he knew that it wouldn't ease the pain in any way. So instead, he just sat there silently waiting for Jimmy to say something, anything. After a minute or so, Jeffrey looked over to make sure his friend was still breathing, but all he could see was the fuzzy air in front of Jimmy's chest, like his soul was ready to take leave.

"What in the world are you staring at?" Jimmy asked.

"Nothin'," Jeffrey replied. "Just makin' sure you were still breathing."

"Yeah, I'm still breathing!" Jimmy yelled. "You think I'm gonna let some little unimportant girl ruin me like that!"

Jimmy ripped the gearshift into drive, slammed his foot onto the gas pedal, and yanked the wheel to the left. They were motionless for a few seconds as the massive engine of the '69 Camaro roared and the wide, fierce tires slung dirt and grass for ten yards or more. The muscle car slowly began to rotate, and then suddenly it yanked itself around and dug into the pavement animal-like.

Jimmy and Jeffrey continued to skid and slide along the narrow road until the monster finally adjusted itself and accelerated at an incredible rate. They were up to 90 miles per hour within seconds as a curve in the road approached rapidly.

"See, life is like this!" Jimmy yelled with madness in his eyes.

"Like what?" Jeffrey asked as he quickly reached for his seat belt.

"Full of unexpected turns!" Jimmy screamed before yanking the wheel to the left and skidding through the harrowing curve. Then, he dropped the pedal to the floor again, causing the engine to roar barbariously. "And then, just when you think you're smooth sailing again…*whooom!*" Jimmy's voice shook the air as he skidded through another, more extreme turn, this time yanking the emergency brake to power-slide through. "You see, Jeffrey boy! It's only by reckless endangerment and a little luck that any of us make it at all."

Unfortunately, their luck ran out at that very moment. Coming out of the curve, Jimmy never fully regained control of the car. Like motion-sick kids on a fair ride, he and Jeffrey spun around and around with blank, expressionless faces. It wasn't until they had slammed into a guardrail and fully stopped for a few seconds that they were able to comprehend what had happened.

They checked and double-checked their entire bodies with methodical eyes, scanning to find any cuts, scrapes, or protruding bones. After finding not a single scratch anywhere, they looked at each other in amazement.

"I can't believe it," Jeffrey said.

"Looks like we were saved by angels or something, don't it?" Jimmy questioned. "I don't think my body moved the entire time, even when we hit that freaking guardrail."

"Mine, neither," Jeffrey resumed. "I don't remember the seat belt locking or grabbing the dashboard with my hands or anything like that."

"Must be a miracle." Jimmy's face was quiet and serious. "I told you God was on our side despite all this stuff we do."

"Yeah, you might be right," Jeffrey replied. "But we can talk about that later. We gotta get the heck out of here before the cops show up."

"Yeah, you're right!" Jimmy's words faded as he jumped out of the car. "All these drugs on us…liquor bottles in the car… drunk driving!" he mumbled as he waited on Jeffrey to cross the front seat and exit on Jimmy's side since his own door was jammed against the guardrail.

They jumped the railing that had impeded their progress and most likely saved their lives, and steamed uphill into the woods. Once they reached the top, they could hear the sirens wailing down the curvy and narrow Dahlonega roads.

"So, whatcha gonna do about your car?" Jeffrey asked.

"I don't know, probably report it stolen," Jimmy despondently replied. "But that's so typical and suspicious-looking. Plus, it's not original at all." Jimmy reflected silently for a moment. "Oh!" he suddenly shouted as his eyes perked up. "I got it. I can say that after I crashed, I was so dazed and incoherent that I wandered into the woods and passed out… ahhhhh, only to emerge triumphantly tomorrow or the next day without injury kinda like Bruce Willis in *Unbreakable*."

"You know, that story would be cool," Jimmy continued.

"And they'll never know I had been drinking 'cause check it out." Jimmy showed Jeffrey all the liquor bottles he had stashed in his jacket pockets on the way out of the car.

"You sure you got all of 'em?" Jeffrey asked.

"Yep," Jimmy replied, smiling confidently. "Here, there's two of 'em that aren't even cracked open yet." He handed Jeffrey the bottle they had been drinking out of and one of the unopened ones. "You definitely have all your stuff on you, right?"

"No doubt," Jeffrey resumed. "Weed and coke, same pocket. Speaking of which…" Jeffrey shifted his hand back and forth, making sure to grab the right sack. "Let's stop and hit some bumps real quick. You got your license on you?"

"Nope, left it in the car, but I got something better." Jimmy searched his pockets, as well. "Check it out, my elementary school library card."

"You serious?" Jeffrey asked as he grabbed the bright yellow card, which was surprisingly in mint condition. "I swear, I learn something weirder about you every day."

"I've always got something up my sleeve," Jimmy replied proudly. "Truthfully speaking, though, this card has brought me good fortune throughout the years. I know this type of thinking is just superstitious crap, but I keep it anyway because, I'm telling you, man, as soon as I got that library card, schoolwork got easier, my athleticism, even though it wasn't much, kicked in, I hit a major growth spurt…shoot, girls even started liking me. Just hold it for a minute real tight and make a wish."

Jeffrey didn't know quite what to do. He looked at the card, then at Jimmy, and then at the card again. Jimmy held the most serious look on his face for as long as he could, then busted out laughing. "Man, I'm just makin' up stuff…hit that bump and come on. We probably need to get the heck out of here just in case the cops want to comb the woods or something like that."

Jeffrey snorted a huge pile of powder suspended on the edge of the card. "See, it's better to do it all in one huge bump instead of wasting time with all those little, bitty molehills," he said before slightly choking on the drainage. After handing Jimmy the sack and the lucky card back, Jeffrey cracked the bottle of tequila and took a big swig.

"Shoot, I can call my brother to come pick us up," he said, surprised by the fact that it took so long for the idea to emerge. "He won't care about us being drunk or high or wrecking your car or anything like that. And then we can just stay at my old house until we figure something out." He pulled out his cell phone to call, but he had no signal. "Jimmy, see if your phone has a signal out here," Jeffrey said.

"Left it in the car, man…didn't even want to look at it any-more," Jimmy replied in a nasally voice as tied up the sack and handed it back to Jeffrey.

"Dang, that means we'll just have to walk until we find a signal," Jeffrey said in frustration. "Well, man, I guess we'd have to walk anyway, so it doesn't matter."

"True, true," Jimmy resumed. "We might as well make the best of it."

"Hey, at least we're not lost in those hillbilly woods up at Stone Mountain," Jeffrey said with a smile on his face.

"Heck, yeah, cheers to that!" Jimmy shouted. "Man, that was awful…just awful. I remember…never mind, I don't even wanna think about it."

Jeffrey started laughing at the frightened expression on Jimmy's face, as if they were still back in those woods—two small adolescent boys trying to muster the courage to go on, having to face the possibility of death with bravery. "Hey, I think I have some papers," Jeffrey said while searching his pockets. "We could smoke a joint."

"Oh no!" Jimmy spoke with a comedic intensity. "I think that's what got us lost in the first place way back when. Whooooooo!" Jimmy shook his shoulders rapidly to get rid of the tingling in his spine. "That memory gives me chills just thinking about it."

Jeffrey laughed again as he watched Jimmy struggle to get rid of the snowy thoughts that were haunting him. "Well, I hate to ask this, but…do you know which way we need to go?"

"Luckily, this time I do," Jimmy replied. "For sure."

"Good," Jeffrey resumed. "That's the best news I've heard all day…well, besides you bringing the liquor bottles with you when we hit the woods. That was pretty sweet!"

The next major road was only about an hour's walk ahead of them. During their unexpected hike, Jimmy was unusually quiet. Unable to chase the envious and stomach-turning images of Molly and that other guy out of his brain, he occasionally began rambling on and on about some funny incident that had happened when he and Jeffrey were in high school or some other happy time when they were building castles in the sandbox or hanging from monkey bars, but in the end, his ramblings would stop abruptly and he would return to the catastrophic, yet unavoidable subject of Molly.

Meanwhile, Jeffrey was growing increasingly worried about Jimmy. He had never seen his easygoing, constantly-joking, always-looking-on-the-bright-side friend flip out like he did earlier in the car. Jeffrey would have never imagined that the world and all the slimy stuff that trailed behind it could make

Jimmy stumble and falter. Nevertheless, here he was, swiftly falling apart chunk by chunk right in front of Jeffrey's eyes as he pulled on the Newport in his mouth, mumbled something into the exhaling smoke, then took a swig from his bottle of tequila.

Jeffrey felt a cluster of anxious thoughts rush through him like an angry, amped-up mob. *It's not supposed to happen like this*, Jeffrey thought. *Not to Jimmy*. He pulled the coke out of his pocket and asked Jimmy for his library card. He scooped up the most that he could onto the corner, shoved it up his nose with a sweep, then handed the card and the sack to Jimmy.

*I hope he doesn't try something stupid and reckless like I did when my parents died*, Jeffrey pondered. Panic began to creep into Jeffrey's chest, slowly filling in around the edges, then the center, progressing toward the top. *This is all too much*, Jeffrey thought.

～ **12** ～

Once he knew the panic was there to stay, Jeffrey closed his eyes and forced his head back until his spinal cord would bend no further. Sticking his chest out like a small bird, he filled his lungs with several deep breaths of air, holding the last one in, then releasing it very slowly. "Serenity now," he exhaled with the last bit of carbon dioxide that exited his mouth.

*Dang, that never does work!* he thought as he leveled his head and opened his eyes upon a forest that seemed to have changed drastically within the last few seconds. The trees, which before had been plush green and fully figured, now appeared to have long, bare, lanky limbs, each one ending in a hand-shaped formation with twisted, wicked fingers hanging down—wicked, demonic fingers that looked as if they were waiting for the call to harvest Jimmy's troubled and bewildered soul.

A little shaken by this image, Jeffrey rapidly seized the bottle of tequila in his pocket and turned it up full blast. The few remaining shots were gone within seconds, but the empty bottle reflected no change in the gloomy scenery. He violently hurled it into the forest, which mocked and haunted him with lanky limbs and wicked fingers hanging down, twisted in hand-shaped formations.

Then, Jeffrey peered into the distance, looking for a road that curved and knifed through the forest, but all he could see was tree after tree. With his frustration and anxiety building to a crescendo, Jeffrey fumbled in his pocket for the second bottle of liquor that he was carrying while simultaneously yanking out his cell phone hoping to find a signal somehow, somewhere.

"Why are you chugging tequila and acting so fidgety all of a sudden?" Jimmy asked.

Jeffrey turned to answer him, but his words never formed. He saw in Jimmy the same dazed, striving-to-compose-himself look that he himself had possessed after the death of his parents.

"It's just a matter of time before we both crack," Jeffrey suddenly, unconsciously blurted out. "Hold up, I've finally got a signal!" Jeffrey was thrilled at the prospect of finding a ride and getting out of the forest. "If my brother answers, do you think you can tell him what road we're headed toward and when we'll get there?

"Yeah, definitely!" Jimmy replied. "I can narrow down the spot and time to within half a mile and two minutes…that way he won't have to ride up and down the road a hundred times trying to find us."

"Good," Jeffrey returned with relief. "Hold up, here he goes. Hey, William, what's up, man?

"Not too much," William answered. "Just sittin' here at work…a little bored, to tell you the truth."

"Good," Jeffrey resumed. "I mean, not good that you're bored, but good that you're not too busy 'cause I need a small favor."

"Okay, shoot," William replied.

"Me and Jimmy," Jeffrey began to explain, "are stranded in the woods somewhere in Dahlonega. We've been walking a while and are almost at some state road, I think. Could you pick us up when we get out of the woods?"

"Yeah, that's not a problem," William answered. "It's actually a good excuse to leave work…but…so, where will I pick you up…and when?"

"Oh, Jimmy can tell you all that," Jeffrey replied. "He knows exactly where we are. Here he goes." He handed Jimmy the phone and cracked open a bottle of Crown Royal.

Jimmy never had a chance to respond to Jeffrey's disquieting comment about both of them cracking, nor did he want to. Instead, he grabbed the phone and discussed directions, arrival times, plans—much lighter and more comfortable topics to address.

In the meantime, Jeffrey scrambled through his past, frantically searching for something in addition to the alcohol—an idea, a theory, an experience—anything that would grant him superiority over the worry and fear that had temporarily captured his mindset. Within seconds, Jeffrey came up with a very promising solution. After all, much of his youth had been spent overcoming similar bouts of emotional instability.

Jeffrey briefly recalled the months leading up to his junior year in high school. Until that summer of love (as he liked to call it), the monthly psychiatric sessions and medication cocktails had proven to be very effective.

His teachers—along with every other adult he came into contact with—constantly ranted about how well-adjusted, polite, and calm he had become. But at the end of July, Jeffrey, without any announcement, cut his medication intake in half, and a few weeks later stopped taking it completely. He was worried to find just how fast and violent the pendulum might swing back.

Coincidentally, Jeffrey hit a major growth spurt at the exact same time. As his body lengthened and his muscles developed, he was surprised to find strength in his limbs and agility in his steps. He was also surprised to find that some of his father's most handsome features—his strong jawline, broad face, and alluring smile—began to surface in his own countenance like a lost treasure chest, freed from constraint, rising to the crest of a calm sea.

These physical transformations not only helped to quell the waves of depression and anxiety, but they also created, in Jeffrey, a hardline vision of his supremacy and superiority. A physical and mental Bruce Banner-like transformation easily freed Jeffrey from his numb, medicated state and the dreariness of his own mind, causing him to crash into his junior year with massive rejuvenation and almost overaggressive behavior.

So Jeffrey, like a conqueror bent on destruction, raised his chin and peered across the weak forest with angry, piercing eyes. There wasn't a single lanky, twisted tree limb that he couldn't break in half with the smallest effort. He was brimming with confidence again, feeling, almost knowing, he had complete control over his mind and all the crooked tricks it had in store for him.

He asked Jimmy for the yellow card and pulled out the sack of coke to celebrate. *I will haunt this forest*, he thought. *I will unleash the demons in my head to roam through its woods. I will bend, break, and burn plant after plant, limb after limb, leaf after leaf. I will trample all this twisted, wicked, evil.* Jeffrey's confidence was renewed. *But what about Jimmy*, Jeffrey resumed. *What can I possibly do? Will I leave him behind? Not possible.*

"All right, it's set." Jimmy handed the phone back to Jeffrey. "He'll pick us up in about twenty minutes."

"Twenty minutes?" Jeffrey asked with excitement. "That's it?"

"That's it," Jimmy responded. "We'll be out of here before you know it."

"All right!" Jeffrey yelled before shoveling a corner full of coke up his nose. "Here ya go." He handed Jimmy the sack and the lucky card, then took a quick survey of their surroundings, trying to determine…but the answer was not to be found in the trees or the leaves or the underbrush, all of which appeared the same everywhere he looked.

Realizing this, Jeffrey turned and stared at Jimmy strangely as he watched him fumble with the card and the sack, all the while laughing at his own clumsiness. *Maybe he's not as bad off as I thought*, Jeffrey thought. *He can't be…smiling like that… right?*

"I've been thinking," Jimmy said timidly before a long pause.

"About what?" Jeffrey asked curiously. "You can tell me anything, man. Come on. About what?"

"About quitting all this stuff," Jimmy answered. "It just seems like I'm stuck inside of a circus or something. Shoot, I can't even tell you what day it is today. It could be Friday or freakin' Wednesday for all I know…man, I haven't even been to my own club, the one I'm supposed to be running, in weeks."

"Well, that makes sense, then," Jeffrey responded. "Quitting, I mean. It seems like the only option at this point. I tell you what…I'll quit with you." Jeffrey couldn't catch himself before saying it. He dreaded those very words coming out of his mouth. "I mean, why not?" Jeffrey continued miserably. "It definitely can't hurt. It's not like my life is running smoothly, either. We'll just have to find other stuff to do that doesn't involve drinking or doing coke."

"Or just not hang out at all," Jimmy responded with a sad,

quiet voice. "Don't get me wrong, you're my best friend, but you're also…I don't know what to call it…a drug-use partner. Man, that's not a good way of puttin' it. Let me start over. I love you to death, man, but me and you…we're bad influences on each other. I mean, honestly, could you imagine hanging out with me and not wantin' to get drunk and high?"

"I can't," Jeffrey answered. "You're right." Dejected, he looked down at the ground and shook his head slowly from side to side.

"I'm not talkin' about forever, Jeffrey," Jimmy assured him. "We'll be able to hang out again…just not right now, not until we both get a handle on this disastrous lifestyle that we've begun." Jimmy was very conscious of the fact that he carefully and clearly avoided the word *addiction*. "We'll probably be able to hang out again in a few weeks…a month at the most."

"Yeah, I understand." Jeffrey was still staring at the ground. "I guess that might work out better for both of us anyway, time-wise." He swallowed and stomached most of the emotions that were trying to burst forth, then looked at Jimmy. "I'll have a lot more time to concentrate on my school stuff, to try to get back in the groove of things. And maybe I'll be able to convince Julie to come back. It hasn't really been that long since she cussed me out and told me…well, I forget what she told me."

Jeffrey began to show signs of hope. He smiled as he imagined scattered lambs scurrying back to their master, and cosmic chaos evolving into ordered galaxies filled with asteroids, comets, moons, planets, stars, and black holes. "And you'll have a lot more time to concentrate on Jimmy's Blues. It shouldn't be too hard to get that place back on track…just book some real well-known singers for the next week or so. And maybe, just maybe…well, no, I'm not gonna say that."

"Not gonna say what?" Jimmy asked. "Probably something about Molly, huh?"

"Yeah," Jeffrey answered. "I was thinking that there's always the chance that she might not marry that guy, that maybe you could convince her to leave him or whatever."

"To tell you the truth, buddy," Jimmy returned, "I was trying not to think the very same thing, but like you said, it is a possibility."

"Yep," Jeffrey spoke with hope as he looked up at the sky. "It is a possibility. All of it."

"You know what else?" Jimmy tentatively said.

"What?" Jeffrey responded.

"Man, to be completely honest with you, I've been reading the Bible lately. I had heard good things about the book of Psalms so I started there, right in the middle. Psalm 23 really jumped out at me. It said this: 'The Lord is my shepherd; I shall not want. He maketh me to lie down in green pastures; he leadeth me beside the still waters. He restoreth my soul; he leadeth me in the paths of righteousness for his name's sake. Yeah, though I walk through the valley of the shadow of death, I will fear no evil, for thou art with me; thy rod and thy staff they comfort me. Thou preparest a table before me in the presence of mine enemies; thou anointest my head with oil; my cup runneth over. Surely goodness and mercy shall follow me all the days of my life, and I will dwell in the house of the Lord forever.'[4]

"I started thinking," Jimmy continued, "I might want to be like David, walking by the still waters, lying down in green pastures, at peace with everything. It sure beats this." Jimmy's head was downcast, and he was almost crying. He was silent for a few seconds and then spoke up again. "I may find my way into a church nearby...just to get things into perspective."

"That might not be a bad idea," Jeffrey returned.

"Just a thought," Jimmy added. "So what do you wanna do tonight? I mean, we've got all this coke and weed left."

"We're definitely not gonna throw any of it in the garbage or flush it down the toilet," Jeffrey interrupted. "It gives me chills when I see that type of stuff in movies. Shoot, I might have a stroke or breakdance into seizures if I saw something like that in real life. So…I guess there's only one thing we can do with it."

"Exactly!" Jimmy said cheerfully. "Think about this—we'll be getting drunk and high in order to celebrate our future sobriety. Ironic, don't you think?"

"Ironic, symbolic, metaphoric," Jeffrey replied. "It's all the same to me as long as we get some more liquor on the way home…and maybe some more coke." He then looked preoccupied, as if he had heard a strange sound deep in the woods. "On second thought, we should wait on the coke. I don't think my brother would be too cool with driving us to…well, you know. Anyway, we've got plenty for now…maybe we can get somebody to deliver some later tonight."

"Yeah, definitely," Jimmy resumed. "That won't be a problem…not a problem at all. All right, we're fixin' to cut through the woods right…let's see…right here." He pointed to a small trail that meandered through the thick underbrush. "Now, watch. We'll be out of these woods in approximately four minutes and…and if William left when I told him to, we'll be on our way to your house within seven minutes. If you don't believe me, then go ahead and start counting: one Mississippi, two Mississippi, three—"

"Okay, I believe you," Jeffrey interrupted with a chuckle. "There's no need to count Mississippis like we're playing hide-and-seek."

"Oh! Look, everybody!" Jimmy raised his arms and shouted to an imaginary crowd. "A man that's too good for us primitive folk who count in Mississippis and play hide-and-seek! Well, maybe we'll just have to count in thousands—one, one thousand, two, one thousand, three…"

"Man, stop." Jeffrey began to laugh out loud. "Tryin' to paint me in a bad light with all these reputable people watching. I can still count in Mississippis and play hide-and-seek! Shoot, I'll even play one potato, two potato if it comes down to it!"

Jimmy laughed. "One potato, two potato," he mumbled, then looked at Jeffrey with a smile.

William picked Jeffrey and Jimmy up along the side of the road within a minute of them hitting the pavement. Jimmy didn't say a word about the miraculous timing, which made the whole thing even more mysterious. He merely smiled at Jeffrey and then turned his eyes upward to catch one last glimpse of the treetops before climbing into William's truck. How Jimmy had calculated their exit from the woods so accurately was something that would puzzle Jeffrey for a long, long time.

William was baffled over the matter, as well. With his thick, dark eyebrows bunched tightly together and his mouth slightly upturned, he stared out the window for a moment at a long row of trees that suddenly looked very somber and mysterious, and then fixed his look on Jeffrey, whose face appeared just as contorted as William's and revealed an equal amount of stupefaction, if not more.

However, the wonder only lasted for several seconds before Jimmy began telling funny stories about some of the girls he had dated in the past and some of the weird situations in which he had found himself. *Drugs and crazy stories*, William thought, *always seem tied at the waist.*

William and Jimmy's voices soon became little more than background noise as Jeffrey drifted into his own universe, as habit would have it. *The last night*, Jeffrey thought to himself. *The last night…and then maybe sobriety forever.* He took a deep breath and began to stare warmly out of the window, thankful for the friend that was wrapped up nice and cozy within his left pants pocket.

*How will I ever give this stuff up?* Jeffrey wondered. *Burst into tears and fall to my knees while "Yesterday" plays in the background? Or will I plunge into a long state of depression and look upon my life with hopelessness and frustration as "Estranged" reverberates in the foreground? No, way too dramatic. That only happens in movies. I will fall apart, though. I will fall apart silently. No song will play. No mermaids will sing.*[5]

*No one will notice or care,* Jeffrey continued to think. *Such gloomy thoughts. Can I stay clean and function normally again—go to class, do my schoolwork, maintain a healthy relationship with Julie, if I can even convince her to come back? Or will I fall off the wagon as soon as I hit a bump in the road? Seems like a bit of a guessing game. Dangerous, treacherous. Like walking upon the thin ice of modern life.*[6] *Like listening to the still, sad music of humanity.*

⧸13⧹

"I'm not gonna lose it," Jeffrey whispered to himself as he stared at the horizon. Large, booming clouds stretched across the sky. A blissful dinosaur here, a happy dog there, the clouds produced at least a dozen mixed images, all of which seemed cheerful and exuberant on such a beautiful day at the beach. William, along with his wife, Calista, and three-year-old son, Jamie, drifted along the water's edge while Jeffrey sat on a towel in the sand.

They had invited Jeffrey to come along on their family vacation to Panama City Beach to get away from his adverse situation in Atlanta. They knew all about the drugs, the drinking, his school situation, his mental instability, and the all around tough time he was having with everything. They had hoped that after being clean for two months, things would turn around for Jeffrey, but this was not the case.

He was still struggling to simply wake up and function on any given day. It seemed the drugs had merely masked the real problem, an intense depression that was dogging and shadowing him through the dark, fearful nights and the wearisome, monotonous days.

Nevertheless, he did have moments of happiness, small bright snapshots in an overall gloomy day. This was one of those moments, as he sat watching his young nephew splashing his feet in the water at the edge of the sand. Jamie splashed and laughed and danced, then did it all over again as if each time was the first. He was a tiny boy with dark brown hair parted a little to the side.

His large brown eyes and pudgy little nose lent a lot of personality to his small, circular face. With chubby legs and tiny feet, he stumbled along the edge of the water like most toddlers barely catching his balance with each step. One step, two steps, splash, he repeated several times before falling on his butt in the sand. He laughed at this, as well.

"You okay, Jamie?" Calista asked before helping him up and steadying him for the next splash and dance. As she stood behind him, her long, flowing, black hair brushed against her shoulders. Her tan skin, highlighted by the blue-and-white-striped bikini that she wore, glistened in the beautiful sun. With a round face, a small nose, and small lips, she exuded beauty and grace with every little smile and joyful laugh. She glanced at Jeffrey with her piercing brown eyes and grinned happily before refocusing on the child stumbling beneath her.

William, a handsome man of pale complexion, was staring off into the distance. His large brown eyes squinted and refocused several times before finding the jet skis for which he had been searching. "Honey, look at the jet skis jumping the waves. You wanna try that?"

"No thanks," Calista responded while staring at his tall frame and well-built muscles. *A strong man*, she thought as she admired him from afar.

"Come on, baby! It'll be easy," William joked. "Jeffrey might wanna try. Whatcha think, Jeffrey?" he shouted across the sand.

"I don't know," Jeffrey responded. "It seems kinda difficult. Don't you have to practice a good bit on a still lake before taking one of those things into the ocean?"

"Practice smactice," William replied.

Jeffrey laughed. "Yeah, you say 'practice smactice' until you get out there," he responded.

"Jamie can do it, can't you, Jamie?" William said in a playful voice to the child.

"Water...splash," Jamie replied.

Everyone laughed at the tiny boy voicing his opinion over riding jet skis in the ocean. Once the laughter died down, they all stared at Jamie's chubby legs stumbling and bumbling along the water's edge. *Water...splash*, Jeffrey thought to himself as he began to chuckle again. *What must he be thinking? It's just water, and he's so happy. I was like that once...an incredibly long time ago, it seems.* Jeffrey suddenly became dejected. He quickly stood up and looked down the beach, trying to shake the feeling.

In the distance, he could see large groups of people playing volleyball, throwing Frisbees, lying out in the sun, calling to one another across the beach. *Probably drunk out of their minds at two o'clock in the afternoon*, Jeffrey pondered. *Like I used to be...I don't envy them...I don't envy them...the smell of alcohol... their tanned skin glistening in the sun...the cocaine waiting upstairs in the room...I don't envy them...think about something else for goodness' sake.* Jeffrey turned his attention back to Jamie splashing along the seashore.

"Hey, Jamie," Jeffrey said gently as he walked toward the tiny child. "You wanna go in the ocean?"

"Water...splash," Jamie responded.

"That's right. Water splash," Jeffrey returned. "Hey, y'all, can I take Jamie into the ocean if I put a life jacket on him?"

"Sure," Calista responded. "We can all go. Come on, William. Let's take Jamie swimming for a minute."

"Here you go, little boy," Jeffrey said as he softly poked Jamie in his chubby belly. He stretched the life jacket across his back. "One arm, two arms," Jeffrey said as he slid the little arms into the holes. "Now we buckle it in the front. There we go."

"You need a life jacket too, Jeffrey?" William asked with a slight grin.

"Funny guy, funny guy," Jeffrey responded with a slight laugh.

William approached Jeffrey with the same grin and slapped him on the back. "Glad you're here, man," he said softly.

"Me too," Jeffrey responded.

William grabbed Jamie under the arms and picked him up. "You wanna take him in?" he asked.

"No, you do it," Jeffrey responded.

"Okay, let's go," William said. "Come on, Calista."

William approached the water cautiously. "It's probably gonna be cold," William said as he stepped slowly into the ocean. "Whew, it *is* cold!" he said with a shocked look on his face.

Calista and Jeffrey followed closely behind, entering the beautiful blue-green water with the same shock. Once they reached chest-deep water, William stopped. "Probably don't need to go any farther with Jamie," he said.

The waves surged, capped their whitetops, and crashed into the four of them. William held Jamie high enough so that the water would just miss the little boy's face.

"See, this is fun, right?" William asked as he turned to Jeffrey. "Being sober."

"It is," Jeffrey said with a slight grin. *And it isn't*, he thought secondarily.

"You'll get used to it and find better ways to have fun," William returned. "And one day you won't wanna do that stuff anymore."

"I hope you're right," Jeffrey responded.

Jeffrey turned to look down the beach again at the volleyball players, the Frisbee throwers, the sun tanners, the drunk screamers. "Yeah, I know," William said as he caught Jeffrey's eye. "Maybe we should have come at a different time or gone to a different place. I should've known it would be like this."

"It's okay," Jeffrey responded. "I'll be faced with it somewhere, maybe everywhere. I've just gotta get used to it."

"Life is long," William returned. "One day that life you used to live will be a distant memory."

"And just remember this, Jeffrey," Calista added. "Once you give up that life, you can move on and do whatever you want. You can start a whole new family one day, just like William and me, but not with that stuff you were doing or that lifestyle at the other end of the beach."

"That's very true," Jeffrey responded. "I never thought of it that way." *A whole new family*, he thought. *A chance to start over again.*

Calista and William's kindness overwhelmed Jeffrey for a moment. He turned his face away from them in case he began to cry. *They didn't have to bring me on this trip with them*, he thought. *I'm sure I'm a huge distraction…they have to feed me… watch over me…constantly make sure I'm happy…like having another child to nourish.* The tears welled in his eyes, and he began to fight the emotion with everything in his being.

Seeing that they had perhaps pushed him a little too hard, William and Calista backed off of the sober conversation. A quick glance between the two of them indicated that someone needed to change the subject. "Where do y'all wanna eat tonight?" William quickly asked.

"I don't know," Calista responded. "The Pirate Ship would be really fun. You wanna eat at the Pirate Ship, Jeffrey?"

With the rocky emotions quickly alleviating, Jeffrey perked up and turned to face William and Calista again. "Sure, we can eat there," Jeffrey said. "I have a lot of happy childhood memories at that place. What time?"

"In a few hours," Calista returned, "I'll be tired of this beach pretty soon."

"Hey, baby, you wanna hold Jamie for a minute?" William asked with a slight grimace. "My arms are starting to burn like fire."

"Yeah, unless Jeffrey wants to hold him," Calista replied.

"I will," Jeffrey said.

William handed the tiny boy over to Jeffrey and started wringing his arms as if trying to temporarily restore the blood flow to his outer extremities. Jeffrey chuckled for a second at the picture of William shaking his arms like a madman, then turned his gaze back upon the crashing waters and the wispy clouds just peeking over the horizon. He was filled with joy again looking at the peaceful scenery and listening to the little child laugh hysterically every time a wave crashed in upon them.

"This is a nice day," Jeffrey said quietly, almost to himself.

"It's a beautiful day," William replied. "A beautiful day."

"Do you remember when Mom and Dad used to take us to the beach when we were kids?" Jeffrey asked.

"Yeah," William returned. "We had so much fun. You remember that time Dad was trying to show us how to jump real high and dive into the oncoming waves?"

"Yeah," Jeffrey replied. "He dove into a real big wave, and his bathing suit came off." Jeffrey began to laugh out loud.

"He was panic-stricken," William returned. "He was thrashing his hands into the water"—William and Calista began to chuckle—"and looking around everywhere with a real scared look on his face." Their chuckle grew to a roaring laugh.

"He looked for like ten minutes," Jeffrey replied, now roaring with laughter, as well. "And he never could find it."

"And then...remember?" William returned. "Mom had to bring a towel into the water so he could wrap himself up."

"Yeah," Jeffrey replied. "He was so embarrassed. We had to go straight to the room. People were looking at him real funny the whole way."

"Wheeeew," William returned. "Mom and Dad were funny. We must've laughed about that all night."

"They were funny," Jeffrey replied. "Dad was always doing something crazy, or something crazy was always happening to him, it seemed."

"Wheeeew," William returned.

As the laughter died down, the three of them continued to smile satisfactorily. Meanwhile, Jeffrey boosted Jamie up in the air to fly past the incoming waves. Wave, crest, boost, crash...hug tightly...wave, crest, boost, crash. William and Calista, holding on to one another tightly, watched their beautiful baby boy launch into the waves, laugh, and then launch again. His and Jeffrey's happiness surrounded and soothed them like the warm, fresh air blowing against their merry faces.

"Y'all ready to get out?" William suddenly asked.

"Yeah," Jeffrey and Calista said in unison.

"My arms are starting to burn too," Jeffrey added. "I see what you were talking about now."

"That little boy is chunky," William returned. "That's why. Aren't you, Jamie? Chunky, little chubby boy."

"He is a chunky boy," Jeffrey replied while chuckling.

As the three of them waded toward the shore, Jeffrey handed Jamie to Calista and began to faintly shake his arms just like William. The faint shaking soon grew into an elaborate wringing of all his outer limbs, an obvious exaggeration. William looked at him strangely, then began to laugh.

"Now who's the funny guy?" William said.

"That's my rendition of a Harlem Shake," Jeffrey replied.

Upon reaching the sand, Calista set Jamie down and began handing out towels. "Here you go, Jeffrey. Here, William," she said. She grabbed a towel for herself and for little Jamie. "Let's take this wet life jacket off," she said. Then she gently patted him and herself dry. William and Jeffrey did the same, and then all four of them sat down in the sand.

"You wanna build a sandcastle, Jamie?" Calista asked.

"Sand...capsule," Jamie replied.

"No, sand...castle, baby," Calista returned. "Sandcastle. Here's your little shovel and your sand bucket."

"Okay," Jamie replied.

Jamie began to slap the sand with his little shovel, slapping faster and faster with every swing. Then he threw his sand bucket several feet away, yelling "boom" when it finally hit the ground. He laughed and looked at Calista for reassurance. She smiled gently and moved toward him.

"I'll show you what to do," she said while retrieving the sand bucket. "Here, you use your little shovel to scoop the sand like this. Then you dump it into the bucket like this." She scooped the sand up and dumped it into the bucket. "See? Now you keep doing that until the bucket is full."

"Okay," Jamie replied.

"Do you have an extra sand bucket or one of those castle-shaped buckets?" Jeffrey asked.

"Yeah, I think so," Calista returned. "Let me see." She searched her bag for a moment and then produced an almost exact replica of what Jamie was using.

"Good," Jeffrey said. "I'll help him build a sand castle."

Calista handed Jeffrey the sand bucket. He moved toward Jamie, who by now was slapping the sand again with his shovel and slamming the bucket into the ground. "Boom," Jamie screamed before laughing hysterically.

"Or maybe I'll build one for him," Jeffrey said, chuckling at Jamie's playfully aggressive behavior. "Here, watch this, Jamie." Jeffrey quickly scooped a pile of sand into the bucket and repeated the process until the sand bucket was full. Then he flipped the bucket upside-down and slammed it into the sand. "Now the moment of unveiling," he said while slowly lifting the sand bucket.

"Oooh, yay," Jamie said as he looked at the castle-shaped pile of sand. He began bouncing up and down and clapping his hands.

"That's a real sand castle," Jeffrey said with a smile.

"A real sand capsule," Jamie returned. He continued to bounce up and down for a moment, then broke off into a full wobbling sprint. He roared through the sand castle, crushing most of it, then turned to smash the rest of it with his tiny fists. "Boom," he said while laughing wildly.

"He's such a funny little boy," William said, watching from a nearby towel spread out on the beach.

"He's a destructive little thing," Calista added while giggling quietly. "He's all boy. There's no doubt about that."

"You can say that again," Jeffrey added.

"Come here, Jamie," Calista said while patting the ground beside her. "Come sit with me. I have to show you something."

Jamie, still laughing hysterically, wobbled over to her. She gently brushed the sand off his legs, arms, and chest. Then she hugged him tightly and squeezed his little chubby cheeks. "Come sit with me," she said.

Jamie plopped down quickly on a towel in the sand between Calista and William. The three of them instinctively looked at the sky, the gloriously shining sun, the deep booming clouds. They began to look for shapes in the inflated white billows overhead.

"Look, Jamie," Calista said. "A laughing clown. You see it? Right there." She pointed for him to see.

"Oh, look at that one, Jamie," William added. "A puffy dragon. See it? It's right beside the laughing clown."

From his position in the sand, Jeffrey peered into the sky as well, but he didn't see the laughing clown or the puffy dragon. Instead, he saw a happy young man with eyes wide open, smiling ecstatically into the sun. A storm cloud, however, loomed ominously in the distance, as well, making it difficult to determine if the young man would ever reach the magnificently gleaming sun or if his fate would be buried by the heavy, dark shadow.

≈**14**≈

A streak of lightning ripped through the hot Panama City air and smashed into a transformer right off Thomas Drive. The thunder that followed boomed through the modest hotel room, rattling the windows and mirrors. From a chair on the balcony, Jeffrey watched as the clouds emptied themselves and the rain began to pour. They had just made it home from dinner, beating the storm by only a few minutes. Unfortunately, Jeffrey felt the storm arising within himself was not going to be beaten so easily.

Dinner had been pretty straightforward and extremely enjoyable, but just as they were leaving the restaurant, Jeffrey began to feel a slight tinge of anxiety flutter through his chest and follow down into his stomach. Now, alone on the balcony, Jeffrey began to feel the full weight of an anxiety attack barreling toward him. He shifted uneasily in his chair and closed his eyes tightly as his thoughts began to race toward a very dangerous and despairing place. *What am I doing here?* he thought. *Searching for happiness? Am I a fool? There is no happiness…not here…not now.*

The grim, venomous words hissed as they slithered through Jeffrey's abdomen and moved toward his throat. It suddenly dawned on him that within a minute, he would be struggling for air, paradoxically waging war against his own mind and body. He rushed into his room, already feeling slightly short of breath, grabbed two Klonapin along with a brown paper sack, and hurried back out onto the balcony.

As the anxiety set in with full force, Jeffrey covered his mouth with one end of the bag and breathed rhythmically—in and out, in and out...innn annddd outtt, innnn annnndddd outttt—while rocking slowly back and forth in the chair—back and forth, baacckk and foorrthth. His only hope at this point was for the medication to hit his bloodstream within the next minute or so, but that was an empty hope. Jeffrey was no stranger to panic attacks or benzodiazepines.

He knew the anguish had only begun and would last for another twenty to thirty minutes, assuming that the amount of Klonapin he took was enough. If not, he would grudgingly have to take more and more and wait and wait until he ultimately subdued the demoniacal whirlwind and unfortunately anesthetized himself in the process.

*Just breathe and sit,* Jeffrey thought. *Don't need to think about anything serious. Need to slow the heart down. Just sit, be still, and keep on breathing. Don't think about anything ser— There's no doubt that with all of this I'll have to drop my courses again this semester. Good job, Jeffrey. I hope the midterm deadline hasn't passed. I'll get all Fs. I'll never finish school and get a degree. There's no way. I'll never be able to get a good job or a sorry job or any job.*

*How can I work with all of this going on constantly?* Jeffrey continued thinking. *These panic attacks, the depression? What will I do for money, mooch off my brother for the rest of my life? Money will be tight. Relationships will be strained. Just stop, Jeffrey. Nothing serious. Stop thinking. Every thought—negative, cynical, pessimistic, hopeless. I'm ready to get off this ride, but with no suicidal grand finale, it's impossible.*

*Natalie in her skimpy black bikini,* Jeffrey now pondered,

*with hair dripping water cascading in tiny streams flowing painfully over her perfect, soft brown body, waiting, biting part of her lip, waiting and moving closer, waiting, eye contact, waiting, blushing, and looking down, waiting, then nothing. The opportunity of a lifetime, and I did nothing. Driven by unseen winds toward misery. She had such a beautiful look in her eyes, and I…I can't quite remember what I said. It sure wasn't anything smooth or charming. It sure wasn't the truth. I could be with her right now. I could be engaged, setting dates, numbering and naming our future kids. Did I step off the tracks and change my fate? No, fate is unchangeable. This is my fate.*

*I'll never finish school,* Jeffrey pondered further. *I'll never be able to work. Listening to the Piper hiding in the hedgerow humming in my head.*[7] *I fear him. I am afraid. I am a fool. I'm simply adding fuel to the fire, feeding the anxiety. Focus. Just breathe and sit, breathe and sit. Be silent and motionless.* Jeffrey remembered something Eliot had written: *"You know only a heap of broken images, you foolish son of man. These fragments I have shored against my ruins."*[8]

Jeffrey's thoughts wandered and meandered like this into the most frightening and lonely places for nearly thirty minutes before his anxiety began to subside. He whispered a brief prayer of thanks, looked through the thick rain out upon the rolling waves, and lit a cigarette.

He inhaled and exhaled the smoke slowly, enjoying the smooth taste of menthol in his throat and lungs. He closed his eyes and inhaled again as the anxiety-induced fears floated away in the breeze. However, the moment was dampened by the ever-conscious knowledge that an entirely different type of anguish could follow.

Far too heavy to drift away on gentle winds, there was one

thought that lingered on. For some reason, he couldn't shake that brief memory of Natalie. *Where were we, and what were we doing?* Jeffrey thought. *I don't even remember what grade we were in. Definitely not high school. That's as close as I can ballpark it. Seems like something I would remember very well if we almost kissed, though. Strange that I don't remember. Could I have blocked it out all these years? I'm such a fool.*

The regret, the shame, the loneliness it brought produced a quick shot of anxiety in Jeffrey's chest. This was followed by an overwhelming sadness that poured over him. *I deserve to die,* he thought. *How grueling it would be to wait for old age, though. Perhaps something quicker—crucifixion perhaps.*

*No, too honorable a death for me,* Jeffrey continued thinking. *Drowned in a cage. Death by drowning is so figurative and metaphorical, though. Not deserving of such a grand death. Burned alive, maybe. My spirit goes up in smoke, ashes scattered to the winds. Too poetic. Impalement—perhaps the perfect amount of shame, suffering, and ghastliness.*

Calm now, but desperately unhappy, Jeffrey sat as still as he could on the balcony listening to the ocean. *This is life,* he thought. The rain had lightened up quite a bit, and now he could hear the waves crashing one on top of another against the shore. But the otherwise peaceful sound was obscured by his disenchantment with the world, with his fellow man, with his place in society, with everything. *This is life,* he thought.

From his vantage point, he could see a couple running along the beach playing, laughing. He could see another couple grasping at one another, kissing passionately. He could see the lights at La Vila blaring brightly, preparing the way for late-night revelry. He could smell the lust, the drugs, the alcohol in the air. *This is life,* he thought.

His thoughts returned home. *A twelve-pack of beer will hold me over until I…maybe a small bottle of liquor to catch a quick buzz. Nah, a small bottle will be better. Let me get a ten-dollar bottle of Cuervo Gold and a twelve-pack of, nah, an eighteen-pack of Coors Light. Yeah, that's all. Here's thirty, keep the change. Thank you. Have a blessed day.*

One shot, Jeffrey pondered, *two shots…three shots…chug, chug, chug…left turn…right turn…speed turn…tires squealing…straightaway…engine roaring…flyin'…'ppreciate it, man… I'll holler at you in a little while, probably a few hours or so…best part…right now…first hit…goin' fifty-five, steerin' with one knee…using my license to shovel rocks and powder up my nose like a fiend. It takes skill and practice to do that, then to tie the bag up too, all the while still using nothing but that one knee to steer.*

*It must be the thousandth time I've left Big Boy's house and gotten as high as a rocket ship before I ever reached the main high-way,* Jeffrey continued to ponder. *A sack worth a thousand times its weight in gold. Real good stuff this time around…blowed up! Feels like the beginning of a weekend filled with wild keg parties and packed-out clubs. Close my eyes at this traffic light and focus on the rush and euphoria flowing like warm, rapid, smoothly streaming water through my body, brain, and soul. Everything is new under the sun.*

*Whew! Don't think about that,* Jeffrey reminded himself. Holding himself tightly, Jeffrey began to rock slowly back and forth in his chair again. He suddenly became worried that William or Calista might come out on the balcony to talk. He knew Jamie was asleep by now.

*But William and Calista,* Jeffrey thought. *What would I say? Having a bad moment—please leave me to wallow alone in my misery.* He turned around and looked through the glass door to see if he might find them approaching, but they were in the kitchen talking and looking through the cabinets. *Whew! Safe for now,* Jeffrey thought. *Maybe I should get out of here. What do I say? I'm going for a walk?*

Jeffrey stood up slowly and leaned gently over the balcony. The couples were still laughing and kissing. The lights at La Vila were still blaring, and the music had begun to play. *Gotta get out of here*, Jeffrey thought. He turned around, slid open the glass door, and walked briskly across the living room. "Hey, y'all, I'm going for a walk," he said to Calista and William.

"In the rain?" William asked.

"Yeah, it's pretty much stopped raining now," Jeffrey responded. "I just wanna walk and listen to the ocean for a little while."

"Okay," William returned. "Don't forget to take a room key."

Jeffrey nodded his head in agreement, hoping he didn't appear awkward or distressed in any way. He certainly didn't want to trouble William or Calista or make them worry for even a moment. Partially drooping his head in order to hide his face, he walked into the kitchen, grabbed a room key off of the counter, and headed toward the door.

Within minutes, Jeffrey had descended on the elevator, walked through the long corridor, and reached the beach. He stopped for a second to enjoy the cool breeze and the smell of the ocean running up onto shore. He felt like this would be the last time. *This is life…there's nothing left here for me*, he thought.

He held a moment of silence for all of the memories of him and his family at the beach. Reaching back into childhood, he remembered the simple joy he had experienced playing in the sand, lying in the sun, crashing through the water as a child. But now those days were gone. They would never happen again. *What I would give to return to then*, Jeffrey pondered.

A gentle tear rolled down Jeffrey's cheek, and he began to weep. *Never again*, he thought. He remembered the times when he and his brother had built sand castles, hunted for sea shells, dug tunnels, buried his parents in the sand. *Never again.* He remembered the taste of salt water and the feel of the water glistening on his tan arms. *Never again.* He remembered the warmth of the burning sun and the smell of the suntan lotion his mother rubbed into his shoulders. *Never again.*

Jeffrey softly wiped away the tears and began to walk quietly toward the shoreline. He soon passed by the two couples he had previously seen from the balcony. They still appeared to be overjoyed in each other's company. Jeffrey had envied them from afar, but now he began to see them in a very different light. He knew their happiness in this moment was only temporary and that for them, for everyone, the monotony of life must always return.

*Vacation now*, he thought. *But soon awaken, work, lunch, work, home, hello, empty words, dinner, TV, bedtime, then set the alarm to replay track number one. The same thing every day. I wonder how they keep from thinking about that now. The endless work, the empty words? We all must live as we dream—alone within an endless monotonous nightmare.*

Jeffrey tried to brush away the words, but they kept streaming in upon his wandering mind. *All the miserable people. Everyone's radio tuned in to the same cryptic frequency, a frequency that emanates from a station that's been abandoned for decades, as if left for ghosts and demons to plague. I know. I have the same frequency programmed into my radio.*

*Quite depressing really*, Jeffrey continued thinking. *It plays the still, sad music of humanity every second of the day, week after week, year after year. Rather difficult to find, but once discovered, it is impossible to part with. Change radios, change frequencies, it doesn't matter. The tune will find you, and your head will hum once again. It's the Piper calling, but you never realize that until it's too late.*

Jeffrey turned his head downward and covered it with his hands as if he might block the thoughts from coming in or tear them asunder from their place in his brain. *But there is time yet, they say.* Jeffrey's thoughts wandered further. *Time to awaken, time to change, time to hope.*

*There will be time*, Jeffrey continued to think, *there will be time; there will be time. But truly there is only time to mourn and weep.* He remembered something King Solomon had once written: "Everything is meaningless, a chasing after the wind. What has been will be again. What has been done will be done again. There is nothing new under the sun."[9]

Jeffrey raised his head again, lowered his arms, and began to rush toward the shoreline in a desperate, futile attempt to outrun his thoughts. As he approached the crashing waves, he stopped for a moment to listen. There was nothing there, nothing in the waves or the breeze to comfort him. *There will be time*, Jeffrey thought. *There will be time; there will be time.*

King Solomon again came to mind: "There will be a time to be born and a time to die, a time to toil and a time to reap, a time to be wise and a time to be foolish. But ultimately the end is always the same. All come from dust and to dust all return. And I saw that the dead who had already died were happier than the living who were still alive, but better than both was he who has not yet been who has not seen the depressing lives that men lead under the sun. What a heavy burden God has laid on men."[10]

Jeffrey listened again, more sharply this time. There was still nothing, and a feeling of nothingness filled his being. His thoughts—nothingness. His sensations—nothingness.

*We shall do best in life,* Jeffrey pondered as he recalled something Schopenhauer had written, *if, early on, we accept that our existence is a mere process of disillusionment, doomed from the start. We begin as happy children, magnificently oblivious, but end as disenchanted adults, absolutely defeated. In the end, there is nothing left for death to conquer when he comes to claim his prize.*[11]

Jeffrey drooped his head solemnly and began to slowly walk along the beach again. Like a martyr approaching the gallows, he felt as though he were walking directly into the doomed fate that he must now accept as his own.

*Life is meaningless,* he thought as he remembered Nietzsche's words. *Faith is dead. The modern world has lost belief in all values and any possibility of transcendence. Nihilism. Time brings only hardship, only suffering. Our time is a time to grieve, grieve for the lives we lead, a maddening concept.*[12] *And the mermaids refuse to sing. They will never sing to me.*[13]

Jeffrey finally reached the shoreline and suddenly felt the cool water rushing up to his feet, then receding, rushing up, then receding. He longed for the coolness to pour over him, to envelop him, to shroud his ever-burning thoughts.

*Time is a tyrant,* he thought as he recalled Faulkner's writing. *Time is a monster. But even time must meet its end. The bell will soon toll, and the dark diceman will speak. Our brightest hope. The death of life. The death of time. But then there's more time. Endless time. Relentless fury from everlasting to everlasting. Time only to weep and gnash, weep and gnash.*[14]

Jeffrey looked out upon the endless ocean to see the waves rising, dark and powerful, cresting beautifully white on top, and crashing with full fury into the surrounding abyss. The moon was full in the distance. He felt as if he were losing control. These thoughts and these sensations he could not stop. *It's a strange thing, the human brain*, Jeffrey thought. *Who's in charge? Him or me? But he is me. Still, the question remains—him or me? The human mind, very strange indeed.*

*Rebellious,* Jeffrey continued to think, *treacherous, a lover of chaos. Always distracting me with these fleeting, random thoughts. Or confusing me with a panorama of unrelated memories. Or jumping forward and backward in time as if it hopes to link the cloudy present with the foggy past.*

*Or, worst of all*, Jeffrey now pondered, *wandering off with no forewarning to explore strange, dark dungeons beneath the earth. Scary realization, this losing control business. What to do? Nothing I can do? Throw myself at the mercy of the court? Maybe. But whose court? The Worm's? Waters did that. It didn't turn out too well for him, poor chap. He was nearly crushed by that crumbling wall.*[15]

Jeffrey looked back at the happy couples and then down the beach at La Vila. He tried to imagine the refuge that love or alcohol or drugs could provide for him right now in this moment. He dropped to his knees and spread his arms wide in surrender. The waves were crashing in on him, closer and closer it seemed, ready to pound him into submission. He reached for the sky, hoping that God would finally recognize his pain. He screamed like a man in agony, his soul starving for light and life. *What does it take to be saved?* Jeffrey wondered.

Jeffrey's scream rose louder momentarily and then quickly disappeared into oblivion. He closed his eyes. The waves rolled and boomed loudly around him. He knew he could end it all right there. *How strange it would be to die, to be no more*, Jeffrey thought. He stood up and waded into the water.

*To magically drift into the afterlife*, Jeffrey continued thinking. The coolness of the water shocked his senses. *But it is possible*, he thought. He pushed on deeper and deeper. *Just a little longer.* The water began to touch his neck, then his face. *And it will all be over.* His head was completely underwater, and he held his breath tightly. *Forty seconds*, he thought. *A minute at the most.*

After thirty seconds, Jeffrey began to feel the burning, the yearning for air. He dug deep and held out a few more seconds, but suddenly realized he lacked the courage to carry out such a reckless action. He burst forth from the water and consumed a huge breath of fresh air. For a moment, he felt relief, but it was only a physical relief. His spirit was still fraught with peril. He had succeeded in doing nothing. This had all been for naught.

Jeffrey swam toward the shore slowly, letting the waves carry him at times to ease the burden. When he reached the sand, he crawled out of the water on his hands and knees, his head drooping, nearly touching the ground. He was defeated.

He raised his arms and twisted his face in anger toward God, when suddenly and unexpectedly he began to remember some passages of Scripture he had read long ago: "And we know that in all things God works for the good of those who love him, who have been called according to his purpose.... For I am convinced that neither death nor life, neither angels nor demons, neither the present nor the future, nor any powers, neither height nor depth, nor anything else in all creation, will be able to separate us from the love of God that is in Christ Jesus our Lord" (Romans 8:28, 38-39).[16]

Jeffrey was desperate. He opened his mouth to pray, but nothing came out. He didn't know what to say or how to pray. He thought for a moment about the verses that suddenly sprang to mind and thought it very odd that Scripture would suddenly be occupying his mind. *Perhaps this is part of a plan,* Jeffrey thought, just as he had a long time before in a similar circumstance as this.

He rose to his feet and stood still for a moment, feeling the cool water drip from his soaking body. The air was silent, and the moon shone full on his weary face. He questioned the verses that came to mind. He wondered whether God's love could really reach him with all his sin in place. *How must I close this enormous gap between the two of us?* he pondered. *What does it take to be saved?*

Jeffrey stood still for a moment longer and then began to reluctantly walk back to the hotel room, where Calista and William were undoubtedly waiting up for him. He was afraid to face them. He feared he might encounter some sort of judgment for what he had done. *Why am I covered with sand? Why am I soaking wet? What on earth was I doing?* He could hear the questions already swarming.

Jeffrey reached the long corridor, then the elevator within a few minutes. He tried to comprehend what had happened since he left the room, but he quickly gave up and let his mind wander again into unforeseen places. *No battle is ever won,* he thought as he remembered Faulkner again.

*They are not even fought. The field only reveals to man his own folly and despair. And victory is an illusion of philosophers and fools. Man is the sum of his misfortunes. One day you'd think misfortune would get tired, but then time is your misfortune. You carry the symbol of your frustration into eternity.*[17]

*Ding!* The elevator sounded. Jeffrey tried to collect his wits as he exited and rounded the corner to his room. *What was I doing?* He tried to form an explanation for William and Calista. *I decided to take a swim. An odd time for a swim, but still acceptable. And I fell on the sand coming out of the water. Strange, but not incredible.*

He inserted the key into the door and gently opened it. "Hey, y'all," he loudly whispered, conscious of the fact that Jamie was sleeping. "I'm back." He walked quietly down the hallway and into the living room, where he found William and Calista sitting on the couch.

"Hey, Jeffrey," William said as he looked up and leaned forward in his seat. "You're soaking wet."

"Yeah, it was stupid," Jeffrey replied. "I decided to take a moonlight swim."

"Oh, okay," William responded.

"Here, let me get you a towel," Calista said.

"No, I got it," Jeffrey insisted. "I need to change clothes and all that anyway." He slipped out of the room quickly, grabbed a towel from the bathroom, went into his room, and closed the door. *That wasn't that bad*, he thought. *Not too awkward. No major questioning. They didn't even notice all the sand.* He peeled off his wet clothing, dried himself vigorously, dusted off the sand as best he could, then put on some dry, clean shorts and a T-shirt.

Suddenly, Jeffrey's phone rang. H walked toward the outlet in the nearby wall, took the phone off the charger, and answered the call. "Hello," he said, reluctant to talk to anybody at the moment.

"Hello," the voice at the other end responded. "Jeffrey," the man continued, "this is Mr. Weathers. I don't want to beat around the bush or waste time talking pleasantries." The man's tone was serious and somber. "I just wanted to tell you. This is very difficult for me."

"What's going on?" Jeffrey asked.

"This is very difficult," Mr. Weathers muttered. "Jimmy has passed away."

"What!" Jeffrey said in disbelief. "What! You're kidding!"

"No, this is definitely no joke," Mr. Weathers responded. His somber tone exuded a calm sadness.

"How?" Jeffrey asked.

"They think he may have died from a drug overdose," Mr. Weathers replied. "Most likely heroin from the way they found him. He was such a young soul." Mr. Weathers began to cry on the other end of the line.

"He was," Jeffrey mumbled. "And a good soul."

"Well, I felt like you should know," Mr. Weathers responded in a shaky voice. "I'll call you again to let you know about the funeral. Good-bye for now."

"Okay," Jeffrey calmly muttered. "Thank you."

Jeffrey hung up the phone and sat down slowly on the bed. *Wow!* he thought. He stared off into space trying to calmly process what he had just heard. *Why is this happening?* It seemed like everything was crashing in on him, everything at once. *This can't be real.* And yet it was real, the devastating anxiety, the crushing depression, the tragic passing of his best friend.

Suddenly everything in his line of sight was obscured by something like a dense fog that appeared out of nowhere, like an eerie ghost ship creaking and rocking on the open seas or a grisly apparition gliding down the hallway of a mansion belonging to ages past.

Then, out of the obscurity in Jeffrey's mind appeared a pale horse, its rider galloping swiftly with the aura of an unstoppable, infinitely destructive force. So this was it. This was his life, a parade of tragedies. There was no hope, no mercy, no empathy...a total disenchantment with the world.

## ❧ **15** ❧

It was zero o'clock. The air stood still. The wind refused to blow. The leaves on the trees hung silently, hauntingly. The blades of grass, slightly brown, looked to be in a slow process of death.

The sun, obscured by clouds, shone down gently on the gravesite, on the casket suspended in air, on the granite tombstone laid to the side, on the fake turf everywhere surrounding the big hole in the earth and extending into a large tent on the grounds. The crowd sat motionless in their chairs. It seemed like the entire world was at peace, quiet and indifferent. And then the preacher began to speak.

"Brothers and sisters, we are gathered here today to celebrate the life and mourn the passing of Jimmy Weathers, a young man with a passion for the sadness of the blues and an enthusiasm for the happiness he found in his family and friends."

*This is so odd*, Jeffrey thought. *Sitting in this graveyard listening to a sermon about Jimmy. It doesn't even seem real. Such a young, promising guy. This shouldn't be happening.*

"About a month ago," the preacher continued, "Jimmy came to my office in a state of disarray. He was confused about life, the meaning of it, the execution of it. He said he had reached a point of total hopelessness, wrapped up as he was in a constant state of uncertainty and the continuous weight of depression.

"It was on this day that, after talking for half an hour, I shared Christ with Jimmy Weathers. I am happy to stand here and say to you that he accepted Jesus Christ as his Lord and Savior in that very moment. It is for this reason alone that I can give you a message of hope today.

"Jeremiah 29:11 tells us, 'For I know the plans I have for you,' declares the Lord, 'plans to prosper you and not to harm you, plans to give you hope and a future.'[18] The Lord has plans for us. His plans are for good, not evil. His plans are to bring us prosperity and hope.

"Most importantly, His plans do not end here on this earth. His plans include our future, even after death. I can stand here with confidence today and tell you that God has a plan for Jimmy. His death, although tragic, is part of God's plan. Jimmy is now in God's hands and part of His awesome and eternal plan.

"Ephesians 1:3–8 tells us," the preacher spoke again, "'Praise be to the God and Father of our Lord Jesus Christ, who has blessed us in the heavenly realms with every spiritual blessing in Christ. For He chose us in Him before the creation of the world to be holy and blameless in His sight. In love He predestined us to be adopted as His sons through Jesus Christ, in accordance with His pleasure and will—to the praise of His glorious grace, which He has freely given us in the One He loves.'[19]

"Brothers and sisters, God has chosen us. From the creation of the world, in love, He has predestined us to be with Him for all eternity. This is for His own pleasure and to His praise. Let us praise God and find comfort knowing today that Jimmy is part of God's eternal family. He is a son of God, both now and forever more."

Jeffrey wondered if Jimmy had reached the still waters and green pastures for which he had longed. He wondered if Jimmy had found peace forevermore.

"These wonderful passages assure us that God operates in the eternal," the preacher continued. "It is difficult for us to understand this and even more difficult for us to practice it. With all the chaos in this world and the confusion it creates, we often find it is impossible to operate in the eternal. This is why we mourn the loss of loved ones. But God is not mourning today.

"His focus is on the eternal. In God's eyes, Jimmy's life here on this earth was but a brief moment in time. Now that time has come to an end, and Jimmy has moved on to a better life. Let us draw our hopes in the eternal today. For we know that our lives too are but a brief moment in comparison with our eternal fate.

"As we look at these passages together," the preacher continued, "we see that God has many plans for us. Most of these plans are set in the eternal and were put into motion before the foundation of the world. Before we even existed, God was making provisions for us. The greatest of these provisions was the sending of His Son. John 3:16 tells us, 'For God so loved the world that He gave His one and only Son, that whosoever believes in Him shall not perish but have eternal life.'[20]

"God's one and only Son, Jesus Christ, was sent to this earth to die for our sins so that our transgressions would not be held against us. By inviting Him into our lives and accepting His forgiveness, we may gain eternal life, in heaven, with God forevermore. We can have hope today knowing that Jimmy made such a profession of faith shortly before he died. Let us make the same profession of faith, right here, right now."

*So, is this what it takes to be saved?* Jeffrey questioned in his mind.

"Brothers and sisters," the preacher said, "we know that this life is tough and full of burdens, but take heart, through Christ we have an eternity with no more sorrow, no more hardship. In Him, we have redemption through His blood, the forgiveness of sins, in accordance with the riches of God's grace.

"These riches last forever, and they are God's best, for the greatest gift the world has ever known is the gift of eternal life through Christ Jesus our Lord. I have hope today that Jimmy is partaking of these gifts right now. He is sitting at the feet of our Lord and Master, basking in the glory and singing songs of praise to our Father who art in heaven.

"I want to close with the reading of one more passage of Scripture," the preacher continued. "This is a passage that should bring all of us hope as we leave this solemn place and move out today into the world that Jimmy knew so briefly, yet so well. Second Corinthians 1:3–5 tells us, 'Praise be to the God and Father of our Lord Jesus Christ, the Father of compassion and the God of all comfort, who comforts us in all our troubles, so that we can comfort those in any trouble with the comfort we ourselves have received from God. For just as the sufferings of Christ flow over into our lives, so also through Christ our comfort overflows.'[21]

"Brothers and sisters, thank you all for coming today. As you leave, remember that God is our comfort. We do not mourn and wail as the pagans do. We do not grieve as those who have no hope. We can find comfort right now knowing that Jimmy is with our Lord and Savior, Jesus Christ, both now and forevermore."

Jeffrey rose quickly from his seat. He was ready to get far

away from this graveyard, far away from Jimmy's motionless body lying in the casket just a few feet away, far away from the preacher who had just raised inevitable questions of massive significance in Jeffrey's mind and soul.

However, he knew he must speak with Mr. and Mrs. Weathers before he departed. He slipped by several men congregating at the end of his row and found his way to the front, where Jimmy's parents were just rising from their chairs.

"Hello, Mr. and Mrs. Weathers," Jeffrey said as he approached them with outstretched arms. *They look terribly sad*, Jeffrey thought.

"Hello, Jeffrey," they said, almost in unison, as they hugged him one at a time.

"I can't imagine how you must feel," Jeffrey said as he suddenly found the need to maintain his composure. *What an awful thing to lose a son*, he thought.

"This is a terrible time," Mrs. Weathers declared.

"Yes, a terrible time," Mr. Weathers joined in. "But I thought the sermon was really encouraging."

"It was," Jeffrey agreed. "It was a nice service. Peaceful and solemn."

"Jimmy was a special boy," Mrs. Weathers added. "He always was."

"He was a great friend to me...always," Jeffrey said. "Always."

"And you were a great friend to him," Mr. Weathers remarked. "Thank you, Jeffrey, for coming to the service."

"I wouldn't have missed it for the world," Jeffrey concluded. *But now it's time to get out of here*, he thought to himself.

Jeffrey nodded his head and pursed his lips to signal goodbye, then turned to walk away. There were men and women gathered everywhere in groups of three, four, and five with seemingly nowhere to go.

They somberly stood by, talking of Jimmy and the sermon, but mostly unimportant things like the dress one woman chose to wear or their plans for lunch and dinner. Jeffrey dodged in and out of these groups, wondering how they had become so comfortable and patient in life to stand in such a place talking of such things with no ardent desire to flee.

As Jeffrey escaped the last group blocking his way, he heard someone call his name. He turned, thinking that the voice sounded vaguely familiar, and saw Natalie standing there with a compassionate look in her still, watery eyes. They were the same eyes that had dominated Jeffrey's youth, that had always given him the peaceful feeling of home, those beautiful aqua-colored eyes, so like clear, tropical waters.

He was shaken for a moment, but then he gathered the courage to approach her. As he drew near, he studied every aspect of her rosy, high cheekbones, the dark makeup high-lighting her eyes, the hair parted to the side and curly at the bottom, the silky dress lightly gripping her petite figure, the shiny, black open-toed shoes. He wanted to soak in the moment, to stamp into his memory every feature of her being.

"Hello, Natalie," Jeffrey said as he reached out and hugged her gently. *To hold on to her forever*, he thought to himself. *What a dream.*

"Hello, Jeffrey," Natalie returned. "It's been a long time."

"It has been," Jeffrey said. "Much too long." *I would have waited until the end of time*, he thought.

"Terrible to meet under these conditions, though," Natalie replied. "Jimmy was really a great guy."

"He was," Jeffrey added. "He was the best."

"But better to meet now than never, right?" Natalie questioned.

"Yes," Jeffrey answered as he chuckled. "Better now than five or ten years from now." *When it's all over for me*, he silently contemplated.

"You look really good," Natalie said.

"You do too," Jeffrey responded.

"Look, Jeffrey," Natalie spoke suddenly, then paused for a moment. "Look, I've always regretted how things were sort of left hanging between you and me. I've thought about calling you a hundred times, but I didn't have the courage. I felt like I sort of broke your heart a long time ago."

"No, it's okay," Jeffrey replied. "That's just the way things were meant to be."

"But it's not okay," Natalie returned. "I want to make it up to you. Would you like to go to dinner or something sometime soon?"

"Yes, definitely," Jeffrey said with delight. "I would love to do that."

"Okay...good," Natalie replied. "But I can't right now. My mom is expecting me for lunch."

"Anytime would be great," Jeffrey added. "Tonight...tomorrow." *For you, I would wait forever*, he thought.

"How about tonight?" Natalie asked as she pulled out a pen and quickly scribbled something down on a small piece of paper. She handed the paper to Jeffrey. "Here's my phone number. Call me around five or six o'clock and we'll make plans then."

"Okay," Jeffrey said in disbelief as he grabbed the paper from her hand. "I'll call you later."

"Good-bye," Natalie responded as she turned to go. "I'll see you tonight."

"Okay...good-bye," Jeffrey replied. *Tonight*, he thought, *it will finally happen tonight.*

The graveyard suddenly felt very quiet and still, but inwardly Jeffrey struggled to find the peace that usually accompanied such a solemn place as this. Mixed emotions seemed to flow from all directions. Part of him wanted to rush back and grab Natalie, to hold her until the end of time. Another part of him wanted to hurry back and speak with the preacher, to ask him how he might find some sort of harmony and tranquility in this life.

Still another part of him wanted to yank Jimmy out of the casket, shake him until he awoke, and make a path to the nearest liquor store or bar on the corner. He began to walk nervously within the peaceful backdrop, thinking of the multiple directions in which he was being pulled.

*What an odd thing for Jimmy to be gone*, Jeffrey thought. *Just yesterday it seems we were at that club downtown trying to pick up girls, spinning on the dance floor, getting high in the bathroom. I'll have to get high by myself now, but I've done it before. No big deal. Might try it now just for kicks. Call Big Boy, hit that stoplight by his house, get blown right there in the car, be filled with excitement, exhilaration, euphoria.*

*I should just be responsible, though*, Jeffrey now pondered, *and wait for Natalie. Tonight, the date of my life, dinner, nice conversations about our past, our future. Later, maybe kiss her for the first time. Be filled with butterflies, anticipation, and passion. But an even better thing to do might be to go talk to that preacher. Tell him about the depression and the anxiety.*

*Ask him how to be ransomed*, Jeffrey pondered further, *to be set free, to be filled with peace, righteousness, goodness, and love. See the preacher and find the happiness that has mystified me all my life? Go with Natalie and mark out a new future? Get high and hit that bar near my apartment? Get high and burn up the club tonight? Get high and throw it all away?* Jeffrey felt the intense desires floating, fighting, and forging ahead to establish a new future.

## ≈16≈

Jeffrey and Natalie walked slowly down Walker Street SW in Atlanta, Georgia. They had been dating now for a few months. She had helped him get back into the swing of things concerning school and day-to-day life. He had stopped using drugs and alcohol to numb whatever pain remained.

However, something was still missing in his life. He had love and sobriety, but he still felt he needed more. Natalie knew this as well, without Jeffrey mentioning a word. Consequently, she had resolved to take him to a Johnny Alday Evangelical Event at the State Farm Arena that evening.

As they crossed to the left side of the street, Jeffrey looked up at the traffic lights. They were red at the moment, and the cars waited impatiently. The engines purred, and the horns honked. But Jeffrey was oblivious to the traffic surrounding him. He noticed how the lights blurred onto the roadway. He could see the smearing of green at one angle and red at the other.

*This is beautiful*, he thought. He looked at the full moon overhead pouring opaque light onto the Atlanta speedway. Everything looked wonderful, and peace radiated through his entire body. *Perhaps this is a premonition of what's to come*, he thought.

Little did Jeffrey know, he was right. Soon Natalie guided him by the arm into the huge building, where they presented their tickets to the man at one set of double doors. They quickly found themselves searching for a seat high up in the arena, which faced the stage. Solemn Christian music played in the background as they stepped higher and higher.

Soon, they found two open seats near the wall at the top of the steps. They seated themselves and prepared to listen intently to the speaker, who was standing slightly backstage. As the last song died down, Reverend Johnny Alday approached the stage.

"Good evening," Alday said. "We're going to look at Ezekiel 34 and John 10 and at the contrast between the good shepherd and the bad shepherd. The Bible tells us that Jesus is the Good Shepherd. And the Bible tells us that He is such a good shepherd that He has never lost a single sheep. Jesus never loses his sheep."

"Our text will begin with Ezekiel 34.

*The word of the Lord came to me: "Son of man, prophesy against the shepherds of Israel; prophesy, and say to them, even to the shepherds, Thus says the Lord God: Ah, shepherds of Israel who have been feeding yourselves! Should not shepherds feed the sheep? You eat the fat, you clothe yourselves with the wool, you slaughter the fat ones, but you do not feed the sheep. The weak you have not strengthened, the sick you have not healed, the injured you have not bound up, the strayed you have not brought back, the lost you have not sought, and with force and harshness you have ruled them. So they were scattered, because there was no shepherd, and they became food for all the wild beasts. My sheep were scattered; they wandered over all the mountains and on every high hill. My sheep were scattered over all the face of the earth, with none to search or seek for them.*

*"Therefore, you shepherds, hear the word of the Lord: As I live, declares the Lord God, surely because my sheep have become a prey, and my sheep have become food for all the wild beasts, since*

*there was no shepherd, and because my shepherds have not searched for my sheep, but the shepherds have fed themselves, and have not fed my sheep, therefore, you shepherds, hear the word of the Lord: Thus says the Lord God, Behold, I am against the shepherds, and I will require my sheep at their hand and put a stop to their feeding the sheep. No longer shall the shepherds feed themselves. I will rescue my sheep from their mouths, that they may not be food for them.*

*"For thus says the Lord God: 'Behold, I myself will search for my sheep and will seek them out. As a shepherd seeks out his flock when he is among his sheep that have been scattered, so will I seek out my sheep, and I will rescue them from all places where they have been scattered on a day of clouds and thick darkness.'"*

*"'And I will bring them out from the peoples and gather them from the countries, and will bring them into their own land. And I will feed them on the mountains of Israel, by the ravines, and in all the inhabited places of the country. I will feed them with good pasture, and on the mountain heights of Israel shall be their grazing land. There they shall lie down in good grazing land, and on rich pasture they shall feed on the mountains of Israel.'"*

*"'I myself will be the shepherd of my sheep, and I myself will make them lie down,' declares the Lord God. 'I will seek the lost, and I will bring back the stray, and I will bind up the injured, and I will strengthen the weak, and the fat and the strong I will destroy. I will feed them in justice. I will rescue my flock; they shall no longer be a prey. And I will judge between sheep and sheep.'"[22]*

"So the first thing we're going to do is look at the bad shepherds. We're going to look at some of the bad characteristics of the bad shepherds. We see that the bad shepherds feed themselves, think of themselves, love themselves. The bad shepherds also squander the leftovers.

"They are not good stewards of what God has given. We also see that power and influence corrupts the bad shepherds. They devour the land and they cause grief, not only to themselves, but to everyone. They lead people stray. They scatter the weak and the poor and injure others. And they're unable to bring anyone, let alone themselves, into the promised land.

"Now, shepherds of God should feed the sheep, should take care of the sheep. It's a very obvious point to make. But here we find the evil shepherds do not do that. The idea of sharing or personal sacrifice is nowhere to be found. It's nowhere to be found in their practice, but more importantly, it's nowhere to be found in their heart.

"The Bible tells us the heart we must guard above all things because out of it flows everything. We see that the bad shepherds bring forth bad things out of the evil in their hearts. So you see the bad shepherds ignore the needs of others. They care not for the injured. Nor do they seek out the lost. And they also rule in a very harsh manner.

"It's the saddest thing that shepherds who are given the responsibility of keeping the sheep fail to deliver these sheep to safety, unable to protect them, unwilling to care. When the shepherds do not do what they are supposed to do, the sheep are laid bare to the wild beasts that would come and devour them.

"Now we will look at one of the characteristics of good shepherds. Good shepherds are the ones who will risk their lives personally for the sheep. Good shepherds seek and rescue. There are no lengths to which they won't go to find the sheep. They will leave the 99 and will not return until they find the sheep that is missing.

"Next, we see good shepherds gather. They gather and care. Good shepherds are constantly striving to provide for the sheep. Good shepherds provide peace, protection, and strength. Good shepherds make the sheep lie down in pasture.

"Now we turn to John 10 to see Jesus as the Good Shepherd.

*"Truly, truly, I say to you, he who does not enter the sheepfold by the door but climbs in by another way, that man is a thief and a robber. But he who enters by the door is the shepherd of the sheep. To him the gatekeeper opens. The sheep hear his voice, and he calls his own sheep by name and leads them out.*

*"'When he has brought out all his own, he goes before them, and the sheep follow him, for they know his voice. A stranger they will not follow, but will flee from him, for they do not know the voice of strangers…*

*"I am the door of the sheep. All who came before me are thieves and robbers, but the sheep did not listen to them. I am the door. If anyone enters by me, he will be saved and will go in and out and find pasture.*

*"'The thief comes only to steal and kill and destroy. I came that they may have life and have it abundantly. I am the good shepherd. The good shepherd lays down his life for the sheep. He who is a hired hand and not a shepherd, who does not own the sheep, sees the wolf coming and leaves the sheep and flees, and the wolf snatches them and scatters them. He flees because his is a hired hand and cares nothing for the sheep.*

*"I am the good shepherd. I know my own and my own know me…and I lay down my life for the sheep. And I have other sheep that are not of this fold. I must bring them also, and they will listen to my voice. So, there will be one flock, one shepherd. For*

*this reason, the Father loves me, because I lay down my life that I may take it up again."* [23]

"So, the Good Shepherd is the gate and the door. He lays across the entrance and no one comes in or out except through the way that God has designed the passage that the Good Shepherd has provided for all of us who confess the name of Christ. It doesn't matter if you're in the back of the line or the front, there is no reason to be anxious. The Good Shepherd has secured our entrance.

"Your way has already been purchased. It was purchased long ago on the old, rugged cross. You, indeed, do know the Good Shepherd and, more importantly, the Good Shepherd knows you.

"The leaders of the day thought they could do the worse thing imaginable to the Good Shepherd. They said to themselves, 'We'll kill him. Let's just get rid of him.' But God took the worse thing that could be planned for the Good Shepherd, and in His sovereignty, turned it into the very best thing for mankind.

"Because they thought of this evil, to put an innocent man, an innocent shepherd on the cross and crucify him, it became the very way, the very gateway, the very door that provides a way for us to have fellowship with God for all eternity. Through his suffering and dying on the cross, and by our belief in the Son of God on that cross, we swap our sin for The Good Shepherd's righteousness.

"The Bible says that the wages of sin is death and yet the Good Shepherd's death on that cross satisfied God's wrath and took away our sin and ultimate punishment. As Jesus stated, the Good Shepherd lays down his life for the sheep.

"I want to implore you today to fall farther and farther into the arms of the Good Shepherd. I want you to let the Good Shepherd care for you like we have read about tonight. When you allow the Good Shepherd to have provision for you and you trust in the provision of the hand of the Good Shepherd.

"I promise you that if you put your trust in the Good Shepherd, you may not have everything you want, but you will have everything you need. The Lord is the Good Shepherd and if you are His, He will never lose you.

"I want to end with a brief story tonight that has been told with several different variations along the years and serves as a great metaphor for God's desire to see us saved by the Good Shepherd. There was a man who deserted his wife and two kids for alcohol, drugs, and women. He spent five years away from them, living the fast life until it all came crashing down. He knew that he had embarrassed and shamed his family greatly with the sins he committed, but he wanted to come back nevertheless. So, he wrote a letter to his family telling them that he had sinned against both them and God and didn't deserve their mercy or grace but hoped it might be extended to him when he returned home the next Friday.

"If they would accept him again, he said, it would mean all the world to him. So, he instructed them to put out gold ribbons on the door of their apartment building if they would accept him back. On the next Friday, when the taxi carrying the man rounded the corner to his street, there were gold ribbons everywhere—on the street signs, on the shop windows, and all over the light poles. The man was in tears as the taxi stopped in front of the apartment building. After paying the taxi driver, he got out and looked at the street filled with ribbons one final time and then with a newfound hope, walked inside the apartment building. The entire family was overjoyed.

"If you are sitting in this arena tonight and have never been saved, you should know that right now all of heaven is lit up with gold ribbons and banners waiting for you. And the Good Shepherd is standing before his throne ready to give you eternal life. You have a chance tonight to leave the depression behind, to be ransomed from your sins, to be redeemed forever. Will you pray with me the prayer of salvation?"

Jeffrey had been on the edge of his seat for the last few minutes. He crept even farther to the edge as the preacher finished. His opportunity was here. *So, this is what it takes to be saved?* he thought. *To be rescued and ransomed?* As Johnny Alday began to pray, Jeffrey closed his eyes and prayed along with him in silence. *Lord, I know that I am a terrible sinner*, he recited in his mind. *I have sinned and fallen short of the glory of God. Right now, I accept the free and eternal gift of salvation from Your Son, Jesus Christ. I believe that He died for my sins and ransomed my life forever. Thank You, Lord, for the gift of salvation. I invite You into my heart now to save and redeem me. Please fill me with Your Holy Spirit now and help me to move out from this place as a changed man. Thank You, Lord.*

As Jeffrey opened his eyes, he looked over at Natalie. Tears were running down her beautiful face. Her mission was accomplished. Jeffrey had been saved. They rose together and hugged for nearly a minute before descending the stairs and exiting the double doors out into the open air.

A peace and a stillness were radiating through Jeffrey's heart, mind, and body. "Thank You, Lord," Jeffrey whispered. The instant happiness and the overwhelming peace that now reigned in his heart gave Jeffrey hope that his life need not be an emotional roller-coaster ride, nor an infinite string of depressing misfortunes. His eyes had been opened…finally.

# ❧ 17 ❧

A few months later, Jeffrey was seated on the edge of his chair outside on a hotel balcony in Gatlinburg, Tennessee. As he was brushing his teeth a few minutes before, he had decided that the peace found in Jesus Christ our Lord would be the theme of the day. So, as he leaned forward now toward the table in front of him, he flipped to the glossary in the back of his Bible to look up verses on peace.

The first verse he saw was John 14:27. He searched out the book of John in his new, brown leather Bible and began to read: "Peace I leave with you; my peace I give you. I do not give to you as the world gives. Do not let your hearts be troubled and do not be afraid."[24] He read over the verse several times, contemplating its meaning, making sure that he internalized the message.

Then, he flipped to the glossary again. He found that Philippians 4:7 was the next verse listed. He searched for the book of Philippians and found it toward the end of his Bible. He began to read: "And the peace of God, which transcends all understanding, will guard your hearts and your minds in Christ Jesus."[25] Again, he read the verse several times and thought deeply about the message it presented.

When he felt good about his understanding of the concept, he flipped back to the glossary. The third reference he saw led him to Isaiah 26:3, toward the middle of the Bible. He found it and began to read: "You will keep in perfect peace those whose minds are steadfast because they trust in you."[26] After reading over the verse a few times, he internalized this one, as well, contemplating its meaning for several seconds.

Then, he began to pray. "Lord God," Jeffrey said quietly, "please fill me with Your Holy Spirit today and be a powerful force within me. Through Your Holy Spirit, please grant me joy and happiness. Please give me the wisdom to make the right decisions. Help me to exhibit kindness, goodness, self-control, and love. Most of all, Lord, please give me peace and understanding. Thank You, Lord. In Jesus' name I pray, amen."

As Jeffrey finished, he inhaled the cold, dry mountain air slowly and began to rise from his seat. He knew that he was still learning what it meant to be a Christian, but he was certainly making progress in his faith. He put the work in by reading his Bible and praying daily. He did his best to let the Holy Spirit guide and empower him. He followed Jesus' command to love the Lord his God and his neighbor as himself.

For the most part, Jeffrey's depression and anxiety had subsided. His doctor had placed him on some very effective medicine to combat the mental illness that plagued him. And his newfound faith gave him hope for each new day under the sun. He was still tempted at times to use drugs and alcohol, but prayer and what he felt to be the Holy Spirit always prevented him from doing so.

He had started back to school at GA Tech and was doing quite well. He was now carrying a GPA of 3.5, basically A's and B's. He and Natalie were still dating, and they had talked briefly of getting married a few years down the road. His life, in a nutshell, was perfect. He knew that, of course, dark days might come at any time, but his faith in Christ convinced him that he could overcome any obstacle that might be placed in his way.

Most of all, a sense of peace consumed his every waking moment. He felt that peace again as he walked through the balcony doors into the house he had rented for a few days. He had decided to go to town and buy a few things, maybe a new jacket and a new pair of shoes. He was still contemplating just what exactly his plans would be. But he knew he was about to have a great day, no matter how he spent it. He was already dressed. So, he grabbed the keys to his room and his rental car and walked out the front door.

Pretty soon, Jeffrey was winding down the mountain, pumping the brakes and swerving through the curves in the road. He noticed that the scenery was absolutely brilliant. A thick forest surrounded him on every side. Every once in a while, he could see through an opening down the mountain. Lodges, ski lifts, ice-skating rinks, and houses built along the steep embankment flooded his sight. *This is beautiful*, he thought. *I'm gonna live here one day. Bring Natalie, start a family, have a great life. Let my kids grow up in the mountains surrounded by all this beauty.*

As Jeffrey reached the bottom of the hill, he began to think again about Faulkner's reference to God as a dark diceman.[27] *But God is neither*, Jeffrey thought. *He is in no way dark. He is a loving God, who was willing to send His one and only Son to the cross to die for my sins. If He is willing to take special care of the birds of the air and all the rest of nature, as His Scripture states, how much more will He take care of me?*

*He is not a diceman, either*, Jeffrey continued to think. *God does not determine our fate by chance, by the metaphorical rolling of dice. Again, He cares for us and is determined to bring us to Himself by the fate that He has predestined. Everything in God's universe happens for a reason, not by chance.*

Jeffrey's car rolled to a stop as he entered the town of Gatlinburg. *So quaint and picturesque*, he thought. *The little stores positioned alongside the grand mountain range. The ski lifts towering off in the distance above the smooth snow and ice, where people were flying down the slopes at breakneck speed trying desperately not to fall.*

*The ice-skating rink a few miles off was positioned neatly in the valley like a basketball gymnasium,* Jeffrey continued to think. *Such a beautiful place.* He exited the car slowly and looked around, intently trying to absorb the scenery around him. The peace that he felt within his soul was compounded by the tranquil backdrop all around him.

As he began walking through the town, he thought again about Faulkner. *No battle is ever won*, he remembered Faulkner writing. *They are not even fought. The field only reveals to man his own folly and despair. And victory is an illusion of philosophers and fools. Man is the sum of his misfortunes. One day you'd think misfortune would get tired, but then time is your misfortune. You carry the symbol of your frustration into eternity.*[28] Once again, Jeffrey knew that absolutely none of these words were true.

*The battle has already been won,* Jeffrey thought. *Jesus rose from the grave, signaling an eminent victory over all evil. And we need not fight. He has done that for us. It is true that life reveals to us our folly and despair, but these things can be overcome and victory can be obtained through salvation. As for man, he is an unfortunate creature, but we don't have to live unfortunate lives. In fact, we are fortunate just to be alive and to have salvation and redemption at our fingertips at every turn.*

*Furthermore,* Jeffrey continued thinking, *we don't have to be the sum of our misfortunes. Jesus is ready at any moment to wipe our misfortunes away. We are a redeemed people. Lastly, we need not carry any frustration into eternity. Heaven is a place where every tear will be wiped away and every scar will be repaired. When we encounter Jesus face-to-face, our lives will be perfect forevermore.*

But it wasn't just Faulkner whom Jeffrey thought about as he continued walking. It was Eliot, Joyce, Fitzgerald, Woolf, Hemingway, Beckett, Foster Wallace, and others. *All elegant writers,* Jeffrey pondered. *And extremely talented, but so depressing and so misguided.* Jeffrey began to see that everything he had read from modernist and postmodernist literature and all that he had heard from pop music and rock 'n' roll throughout the years had misled him into thinking that life was meaningless and hopeless.

*It was untrue,* he thought to himself. *The whole time…it was untrue. The dark diceman, the sum of a man's misfortunes, the thin ice of modern life, the humming in the hedgerows, and all the rest of it were total fictions.*[29,30,31]

Jeffrey came upon a shoe store and went inside. He needed a pair of warm boots in case he decided to go skiing. There was only a small selection of boots. Jeffrey seized upon the third type that he saw and asked a store worker to get him a size 13 from the back. She swiftly returned with a box containing the boots.

He tried them on, shifted his feet back and forth in front of the mirror, cracked a wide smile, and thanked the woman. "Yes, I'll wear them out," he said to her. Happy that he had found the boots he wanted, Jeffrey approached the man at the front counter with swift feet. He paid, then went back out onto the street.

He began thinking about the modernist and postmodernist mindsets again. This time he remembered various philosophers whom he had been forced to read in some of his literature classes. Schopenhauer came to mind first.

He remembered him writing, *We shall do best in life if, early on, we accept that our existence is a mere process of disillusionment, doomed from the start. We begin as happy children, magnificently oblivious, but end as disenchanted adults, absolutely defeated. In the end, there is nothing left for death to conquer when he comes to claim his prize.*[32]

*What a depressing series of thoughts*, Jeffrey pondered. *But incorrect, again, just like Faulkner. Actually, we shall do best in life if, early on, we accept Jesus Christ as our Lord and Savior. That acceptance of salvation prevents any chance of hopelessness or disillusionment. Jesus Christ is the meaning of hope for the lost.*

*And we need not end our lives or live our lives as disenchanted adults*, Jeffrey continued thinking, *absolutely defeated. There is victory in Christ Jesus. He gives us hope for each new day. Lastly, when death comes, we will spend eternity in heaven with Jesus. As Scripture states, to be absent from the body is to be present with the Lord. Death has no power over us, and we are never conquered.*

Next, Nietzsche came to mind. *Life is meaningless*, Jeffrey remembered him writing. *And faith is dead. The modern world has lost belief in all values and any possibility of transcendence. Nihilism.*[33] Again, Jeffrey thought about how depressing and misguided Nietzsche's concepts were. *Life is full of meaning. We need only accept Jesus Christ as our Lord and Savior.*

*The meaning of life then turns to living for Him, being a witness, being a righteous man or woman*, Jeffrey continued thinking. *The Lord provides the meaning. As for faith being dead, Nietzsche is right in some ways. We as a society have lost our faith. A great number of people no longer believe in God, especially in the United States. But it is estimated that there are billions of Chris-*

*tians throughout the world and millions in America alone. There-fore, faith is not dead.*

*The power of Jesus reigns supreme,* Jeffrey thought as he tried to recall a quote from Napoleon Bonaparte that he had heard in a recorded sermon by Martin Luther King Jr. *I have directed great and powerful armies built upon strength and might,* he remembered hearing. *But long ago Jesus Christ started an army built upon love and to this day, millions will die for him.*

*That is the power of Jesus Christ,* Jeffrey concluded as he victoriously wiped Nietzsche's words from his consciousness. As he continued walking, Hegel, Kant, and Marx came to mind as well. *Ultimately,* Jeffrey resolved, *modernist and postmodernist philosophers were just as misguided as the great literary figures. And dangerous.*

Jeffrey looked up from his reverie and saw a clothing store across the street. He crossed over and went inside. On one of the racks closest to the door, he saw a selection of gloves. He studied the leather ones carefully, but ultimately decided upon the thick cloth ones and tried one of them on. It fit perfectly, so he grabbed the gloves and proceeded to the checkout counter. He paid in cash and went back outside. His trip into town was over.

As he began walking back to the car, Solomon came to mind. He remembered him writing, *There will be a time to be born and a time to die, a time to toil and a time to reap, a time to be wise and a time to be foolish. But ultimately the end is always the same. All come from dust and to dust all return. And I saw that the dead who had already died were happier than the living who were still alive, but better than both was he who has not yet been who has not seen the depressing lives that men lead under the sun. What a heavy burden God has laid on men.*[34]

*There is certainly a designated time*, Jeffrey thought, *to be born, to die, to toil, to reap, to be foolish, and to be wise. But this is not up to us. It is all in God's hands. His plan is perfect, and He's always on time. It is true that we all come from dust and to dust we all return. He's right about all of that, but not about what comes in between.*

*We do not have to lead depressing lives, and the living do not have to be constantly dejected*, Jeffrey continued thinking. *Being dead or nonexistent are not the only ways to avoid nihilism and misery. Salvation in our Lord Jesus Christ is the cure for all desolation, and if we live according to God's plan and the rules He has set forth, everything can be new under the sun.*

Jeffrey continued thinking about Solomon as he walked farther. Solomon, he knew, reached a stage of enlightenment around the time that he finished writing the book of Ecclesiastes. *At the closing*, Jeffrey thought, *of what seems to be a book entirely about depression, anxiety, and a total loss of purpose, Solomon discovers the key to a happy life. He states that the purpose of life is to fear God and keep His commandments. This is the antidote to a miserable life under the sun.*

As he reached the car, Jeffrey smiled at the realization that his life was no longer hitched to the carriage containing all of the depressing material he had read over the years, and even quite recently in the book of Ecclesiastes. He opened the door, got into the car, and put the keys in the ignition before briefly thanking God for his transformation. Then, he began to wind back up the mountain through the forest and the thick snow. When he reached the top and exited the car, his phone rang.

"Hello," Jeffrey answered.

"Hey, baby," Natalie said on the other end.

"Oh, hey, baby," Jeffrey returned.

"How's your day been?" Natalie asked.

"Wonderful," Jeffrey answered. "I had a great quiet time with the Lord this morning. I read a few verses about finding peace. Then, I went into town to buy some boots and a pair of gloves."

"You bought boots?" Natalie asked while trying not to laugh.

"Yes," Jeffrey said. "I know you're about to laugh. But yes, I bought boots." He smiled while trying not to laugh himself.

"What for?" Natalie asked.

"I'm thinking about going skiing tomorrow," Jeffrey returned.

"Oh no!" Natalie exclaimed. "Please don't break your neck up there in Gatlinburg."

"I won't," Jeffrey said. "I'll be real careful."

"And don't be sitting by any cute girls on the ski lifts," Natalie continued. "What do they call them, snow bunnies?" She began to laugh.

"Not a chance," Jeffrey returned. "There's no other girl like you in the world. I won't even look at a snow bunny." Jeffrey began to laugh, as well.

"So, when you are coming home?" Natalie asked.

"In a few days," Jeffrey answered.

"Well, I can't wait to see you," Natalie returned.

"I can't wait to see you, either," Jeffrey said.

"I'll let you go now," Natalie said. "I hope you have a great day, baby. Call me later. Oh, and by the way, look on Amazon for a devotional that you can read each morning along with what you're already doing. You might find it very useful."

"Okay, I'll do that now," Jeffrey responded. "I hope you have a great day, too, baby. I love you."

"I love you too," Natalie said. "Good-bye."

"Good-bye," Jeffrey responded.

Jeffrey entered the house thinking about Natalie. She always brought such warmth into each new day for everyone around her but especially for him. Just listening to her voice or watching her walk across the room still brought up all the feelings he had during his early teenage years. The time he had spent with her since only amplified the love he had always felt for her. "Thank You for Natalie, Lord," Jeffrey whispered.

Jeffrey put the keys on the kitchen counter and looked in the refrigerator briefly for something to eat. He pulled out a loaf of bread and began to make a sandwich. As he neatly placed the turkey on one piece and spread mayonnaise on the other, Jeffrey began to think again about his quiet time that morning.

The peace that he read about was instilled in his new life. This was his greatest evidence that the Word of God was real. Whether he read about love or joy or patience, he could feel all of those virtues inside his soul, but the greatest of these was peace.

The peace he felt each new morning was the best indication of God's existence and love for him. The peace in his soul proved to him that Jesus Christ died and rose again. As he sat back down in a chair on the balcony overlooking the beautiful mountain range, he listened now for the still, sad music of humanity that he had heard for so long.

It was no longer there. *There will be a new music of humanity for me*, Jeffrey thought. *It will be like a new song. Like the amazing grace of an ancient hymn reflecting the life of Christ and His death on an old, rugged cross.*[35,36]

# Endnotes


1 Wordsworth, William. "Lines Composed a Few Miles Above Tintern Abbey." 1798.

2 The Holy Bible. Psalm 16:9–10 NIV.

3 Jeremiah 29:11-13 NIV.

4 The Holy Bible. Psalm 23:1–6 KJV.

5 T. S. Eliot, "The Love Song of J. Alfred Prufrock," 1915.

6 Roger Waters, Pink Floyd, "The Thin Ice," *The Wall*, 1979.

7 Robert, Plant, Led Zeppelin, "Stairway to Heaven," *Led Zeppelin IV*, 1971.

8 T. S. Eliot, "The Waste Land," 1922.

9 The Holy Bible, Ecclesiastes, NIV.

10 The Holy Bible, Ecclesiastes, NIV.

11 Arthur Schopenhauer, *The Essential Schopenhauer*, 2010.

12 Friedrich Nietzsche, *The Complete Works of Friedrich Nietzsche*, 2015.

13 T. S. Eliot, "The Love Song of J. Alfred Prufrock," 1915.

14 William Faulkner, *The Sound and the Fury*, 1929.

15 Roger Waters, Pink Floyd, "Waiting for the Worms," *The Wall*, 1979.

16 The Holy Bible, Romans 8:28, 38–39, NIV.

17 William Faulkner, *The Sound and the Fury*, 1929.

18 The Holy Bible, Jeremiah 29:11 NIV.

19 The Holy Bible, Ephesians 1:3–8 NIV.

20 The Holy Bible, John 3:16 NIV.

21 The Holy Bible, 2 Corinthians 1:3–5 NIV.

22 The Holy Bible. Ezekiel 34:1-16, 22 ESV.

22 The Holy Bible. Second Corinthians 1:3-5. NIV.

24 The Holy Bible, John 14:27 NIV.

25 The Holy Bible, Philippians 4:7 NIV.

26 The Holy Bible, Isaiah 26:3 NIV.

27 William, Faulkner, *The Sound and the Fury*, 1929.

28 William, Faulkner, *The Sound and the Fury*, 1929.

29 William Faulkner, *The Sound and the Fury*, 1929.

30 Roger Waters, Pink Floyd, "Waiting for the Worms," *The Wall*, 1979.

31 Robert Plant, Led Zeppelin, "Stairway to Heaven," *Led Zeppelin IV*, 1971.

32 Arthur Schopenhauer, *The Essential Schopenhauer*, 2010.

33 Friedrich Nietzsche, *The Complete Works of Friedrich Nietzsche*, 2015.

<sup>34</sup> The Holy Bible, Ecclesiastes NIV.
<sup>35</sup> John Newton, "Amazing Grace," 1772.
<sup>36</sup> George Bennard, "The Old Rugged Cross," 1912.

# About the Author

SHAWN MERRITT obtained his Bachelor's Degree in English Literature (with a Professional Writing Option) from Georgia Southwestern State University in December 2003 before moving to the Valdosta State University where he received his Master's Degree in the same subject in December 2009. He is now in the English Literature Ph.D. program at Georgia State University and will graduate at the end of Fall 2022.